THE
ITALIAN
SPAGHETTI
MYSTERY

GEORGE EDWARD STANLEY is a professor of Spanish, Italian, and Romanian at Cameron University. He is a past member of the Board of Directors of the Society of Children's Book Writers and is Secretary of the Juvenile Selection Committee of the Mystery Writers of America.

Dr. Stanley now lives in Lawton, Oklahoma, with his wife and two sons.

THE ITALIAN SPAGHETTI MYSTERY

George Edward Stanley

AN AVON CAMELOT BOOK

THE ITALIAN SPAGHETTI MYSTERY is an original publication of Avon Books. This work has never before appeared in book form.

AVON BOOKS
A division of
The Hearst Corporation
1790 Broadway
New York, New York 10019

Library of Congress Cataloging in Publication Data:

Stanley, George Edward.
    The Italian spaghetti mystery.

    (An Avon Camelot book)
    Summary: Miss Westminster and her singing and dancing pupils accept a summer engagement to entertain at Franco's Famous Italian Spaghetti Inn and Overnight Campground and become entangled in an incredible adventure involving, among others, the infamous Pasta Nostra.
    [1. Humorous stories] I. Title.
PZ7.S78694It   1987   [Fic]   86-20681

First Camelot Printing: January 1987

CONTENTS

CHAPTER ONE

Detour to Poughkeepsie

The black-and-yellow school bus, with MISS WESTMINSTER'S FINE SCHOOL FOR GIRLS OF ELIZABETH, NEW JERSEY painted on its side, headed into Poughkeepsie, New York, and began slowing down.

"Why are we stopping here, Herman?" demanded Merridith Cabot.

"Yeah," said Carla and Marla Evans. "We thought we were driving straight through to Little Indian!"

"Ask Miss Westminster," said Herman. "I'm only the bus driver."

"Because I have a dear, dear aunt who lives here, that's why," said Miss Westminster. "We're going to spend the night with her."

"Ah jus' hate spending the night with relatives," said Augusta Savannah, "even in Georgia!"

"I think we should go on to Little Indian," said Merridith. "Our cabaret act opens tomorrow night at Franco's Famous Italian Spaghetti Inn and Overnight Campground, and we need to practice!"

"I think we should stop," said Fredonia Frey. "I need to buy some more chewing gum anyway!"

"Yeah," said Loretta Dobbins. "I can't sing and dance if I'm not chewing gum!"

"Well, *I* think . . ." began Merridith.

"Girls, girls, please," said Miss Westminster patiently. "We're stopping here in Poughkeepsie because we aren't supposed to arrive at Franco's until tomorrow morning at nine o'clock. If we arrive earlier, we'll have to pay for our lodging. Franco made that quite

1

clear in his letter to me. And frankly, I don't want to waste the money!"

"Well, why do we have to go all the way up to Little Indian to put on our show anyway?" asked Carla and Marla. "Why couldn't we just have done it in good old New Jersey instead?"

"Why couldn't we have done it in Atlanta?" asked Augusta.

"Because Sol Siegel, the famous Broadway producer, got us the booking, that's why," said Miss Westminster. "Sol said that Franco was looking for a class act for the summer. Sol also said that if we did well, he'd make sure we made it to Broadway!"

"O-o-o-o-o-o-h-h-h-h-h!" squealed the girls.

"I thought you'd like that," said Miss Westminster. She sighed deeply and smiled. "Just think what a booking on Broadway would mean to our drama department!"

They rode in silence for several minutes along tree-shaded streets.

"Turn right at the next light, Herman!" shouted Miss Westminster. "It's number 456!"

"Yes, ma'am, Miss Westminster," said Herman.

Number 456 was a Victorian gingerbread house badly in need of repair.

"Is *this* where we're going to spend the night?" demanded Loretta.

"Yes," said Miss Westminster. "Isn't it nice?"

"Ah've jus' never slept in a house that looked like this," said Augusta.

"It looks haunted to me," said Merridith. "I'm scared!"

"Well, it isn't haunted," said Miss Westminster. "I have many fond memories of this house."

"Are you sure this is the right house, Miss Westminster?" asked Herman. "It doesn't look like anybody's home."

"I'm positive that this is the right house," said Miss Westminster, "and I'm also positive that Aunt Millie is here. She doesn't stir around too much anymore, poor dear. After all, she's almost a hundred."

"How old?" asked Augusta.

"Ninety-nine, to be exact," said Miss Westminster.

"Ah don't know *anybody* that old," said Augusta, "even in Georgia!"

2

"Let me go warn Aunt Millie that we're here, girls," said Miss Westminster. "I don't want to startle her."

"Isn't she expecting us?" asked Herman.

"Of course she is," said Miss Westminster, "but Aunt Millie's mind wanders a lot these days. She may have forgotten."

Miss Westminster hurried off the bus and up the walk to the porch. She knocked lightly on the front door once, twice, three times, then waited. But there was no answer.

She rang the bell. *Cling! Clong! Clang! Ding! Dong! Dang!* She waited. But there was still no answer.

She turned toward the bus and smiled nervously at Herman and the girls.

Herman and the girls got off the bus and walked up to where Miss Westminster was standing.

"I guess I'll have to knock harder," said Miss Westminster. She knocked harder. *Knock! Knock! Knock! Knock! Knock!* But there was still no answer. She knocked even harder. *Boom! Boom! Boom! Boom! Boom!* Still nothing. She picked up a baseball bat that was lying on the front porch and started banging it against the door. *Wham! Wham! Wham! Wham! Wham!* There was a tinkling of glass as the door window shattered. *"Aunt Millie!"* screamed Miss Westminster. *"Open the door! It's me, Little Gertie! We've come to spend the night with you!"*

"Little Gertie?" said Fredonia to Loretta. "Is that her first name—Little Gertie?"

The girls all snickered.

But Miss Westminster didn't notice. She had picked up the baseball bat again and had begun pounding on the windows. *Boom! Crash! Wham! Crack! Boom! Crash! Wham! Crack!*

The windows shattered. The frames cracked. The whole front of the house began caving in.

Herman and the girls took cover under the porch hammock.

"Are you sure we should be doing this, Miss Westminster?" shouted Herman.

"I know what I'm doing, Herman," said Miss Westminster as she continued to pound away at the house. "Aunt Millie is as deaf as a doorpost. You have to make a lot of noise. I have to do this all the time. It's a family tradition!" She went back to demolishing

3

the front of the house with the baseball bat. *Boom! Crash! Wham! Crack! Boom! Crash! Wham! Crack! "Wake up, Aunt Millie!"* she screamed.

Sawdust began falling like snow. Swarms of termites buzzed everywhere.

Herman and the girls continued to cower under the porch hammock as the timbers began falling around them.

Miss Westminster continued to scream: *"Open up, Aunt Millie; it's me, Little Gertie. My pupils and I have come to spend the night with you!"*

"All right, you're all under arrest!"

Miss Westminster stopped pounding and turned. The sawdust began settling on her head. Two termites buzzed around her nose.

Herman and the girls peeked out from under the hammock.

Through the dusty haze they all saw the Sheriff. He was standing next to his patrol car. He had a bullhorn in his hand. Behind him was a prison bus and several other patrol cars. Lined up beside it were six Grinning Deputies.

"I said, put up your hands," repeated the Sheriff, *"and walk slowly toward the prison bus!"*

Miss Westminster looked around her at all the destruction. "Good heavens!" she said.

"You've done it now," said Herman with a wheeze as he and the girls crawled out from underneath the hammock.

They all began walking slowly toward the prison bus, their hands above their heads.

"I saw this in a movie once," said Merridith. "We're in serious trouble, but *they'll never take me alive!"*

"We'd jus' never have been arrested in Atlanta," said Augusta.

"It's all a big mistake, officers!" shouted Miss Westminster.

"You're telling me!" the Sheriff shouted back.

"I can explain," said Miss Westminster.

"Tell it to the warden," said the Sheriff.

"Warden?" cried Miss Westminster. "We haven't even been tried yet. I demand to see the judge!"

A Grinning Deputy opened the door to the prison bus.

"Step inside, Grannie Caster," said the Sheriff with a snarl.

"We're taking all of you to the Poughkeepsie Popular Prison for People!"

"Grannie Caster?" asked Miss Westminster. "You must be mistaken. My name is Westminster. Gertie Westminster!"

"Sure it is," said the Sheriff with a sneer.

"It is!" cried the girls.

"It is!" cried Herman.

"You can't fool me," said the Sheriff. "You're Grannie Caster and Her All-Girl Gang. But who's this fellow?" He pointed to Herman.

"That's Herman," said Loretta. "He's our bus driver."

"Bus driver, eh? Well, see me when you get out of prison," said the Sheriff. "I'm always in the market for a good prison bus driver."

Miss Westminster, Herman, and the girls stepped inside the prison bus.

One of the Grinning Deputies got on board and slammed the door shut. "Fasten your seat belts!" he shouted. Then he started the bus and headed it toward the Poughkeepsie Popular Prison for People.

The Sheriff and the rest of the Grinning Deputies followed in their patrol cars.

"Oh, Miss Westminster," sobbed Loretta, "what are we going to do?"

Miss Westminster still had a stunned expression on her face. "This is all a big mistake," she mumbled.

"You're telling us," said Carla and Marla.

"If we had gone on to Little Indian, this would never have happened," said Merridith.

"Don't remind me," said Herman.

"I just don't know what came over me," said Miss Westminster. "Every time I come to Aunt Millie's house, I get the crazies!"

"I wonder if they sell chewing gum in prison," said Fredonia.

"I'll just die if they don't," said Loretta.

When they arrived at the Poughkeepsie Popular Prison for People, the Grinning Deputy jerked the bus to a stop and opened the door.

"Prisoners, step this way!" shouted the Sheriff.

Herman, Miss Westminster, and the girls stepped off the bus.

5

"Prisoners, line up!" shouted the Sheriff again.

Herman, Miss Westminster, and the girls all lined up.

"Prisoners, march!" shouted the Sheriff.

Miss Westminster and the girls marched to the left. Herman marched to the right.

"Where are they taking Herman?" screamed Miss Westminster.

"To the Men's Prison," said the Sheriff. "It's standard procedure."

"See you later, Herman!" shouted the girls.

Herman waved weakly.

"I demand to see the warden!" cried Miss Westminster.

"Hello, there!"

Miss Westminster and the girls turned around. A tall, skinny woman in a dark blue uniform was smiling at them. "I'm Matron Maudie," said the woman. "Come with me. I'm taking you to see the warden!"

"Well, thank goodness," said Miss Westminster. "I am certainly glad that *somebody* around here respects my wishes enough to take us straight to the warden!"

"What wishes, sister?" said Matron Maudie pleasantly. "We always take the really *hardened* criminals to see the warden first!"

CHAPTER TWO

Mama Rosa and the Terrible Crime

"But . . . but . . . but . . ." stammered Miss Westminster.

"But first, you'll have to put on your prison uniforms and then line up," said Matron Maudie. "We're very strict here at the Poughkeepsie Popular Prison for People."

Miss Westminster and the girls put on their prison uniforms and then lined up.

"*March!*" shouted Matron Maudie. "*Hut, one, two, three! Hut, one, two, three!*"

Finally they arrived in front of the warden's cottage. Matron Maudie rang the bell. *Dum-duh-dum-dum! Dum-duh-dum-dum!* A maid answered the door.

"Grannie Caster and Her All-Girl Gang to see Warden Wilhelmina!" announced Matron Maudie.

Miss Westminster paled. "But we're not—"

"Don't worry," whispered Matron Maudie. "The warden's *impressed* by hardened criminals."

The maid led them all into the library and seated them near a fireplace that had a roaring fire in it.

"Boy, it's hot in here," said Merridith.

"Why does she have a fire going in the middle of summer?" complained Loretta.

"Hello-o-o, hello-o-o, hello-o-o!"

Everybody looked up. A stout lady dressed in a powder blue prison uniform stood at the door of the library. She was dabbing away perspiration from her forehead with a blue lace handkerchief.

7

"I'm Warden Wilhelmina," said Warden Wilhelmina.

Matron Maudie saluted and snapped to attention.

"Tea, Phillida!" said Warden Wilhelmina to the maid. Then to Matron Maudie she added, "Matron Maudie, introduce our distinguished guests!"

"Ma'am!" said Matron Maudie with another salute. "I'd like to present Grannie Caster and Her All-Girl Gang! Ma'am!" She saluted again, then marched out the door backward.

"I am absolutely honored by your presence in my prison," said Warden Wilhelmina, taking a seat by the fire.

"We're honored you're honored," said Miss Westminster, "but there's something very important that we must talk to you about right away."

"Don't rush me, sweetheart," said Warden Wilhelmina. "We have all the time in the world." She grinned. "After all, you are really bad, bad girls. But then that's why I'm so thrilled you're here!"

"But that's what we wanted to talk to you about," said Fredonia.

"Yeah," said Loretta, "this has all been a terrible mistake!"

"You'll never take me alive!" screamed Merridith.

Warden Wilhelmina gave her a strange look.

"You see," said Miss Westminster, "I'm not Grannie Caster and these girls are not bad!"

"No!" cried the girls.

Warden Wilhelmina smiled. "That's what they all say!" she said. "But I just want to take this opportunity to tell you that I am absolutely thrilled to have you terrible people in my prison! You've really done some mean things in your life, Grannie Caster. Your being here will give us the reputation we've been looking for!"

"But I've just told you," said Miss Westminster, "I am not Grannie Caster!"

"And we're not Her All-Girl Gang either!" cried the girls.

Phillida returned with the tea and sandwiches.

Warden Wilhelmina looked at Miss Westminster and the girls and then said, "Would you care for some cucumber sandwiches?"

"I'm not very hungry," said Miss Westminster.

"Us either," said the girls.

Click! Click! Click! Click! Click! Click! Click! Click!

8

Warden Wilhelmina turned. "Something's on the teletype," she said. "Will you please excuse me?" She walked over to the teletype machine and tore off the message. She read it. "*Aaaaaaaaaaagggggggggghhhhhhhhhh!*" she screamed. "It says that Grannie Caster and Her All-Girl Gang raided the Utica Unpopular Prison for People ten minutes ago and sprung one of their gang members. That means they're still at large!" She stamped her foot. "Rats! Rats! Rats!" Then she looked at Miss Westminster and the girls. "Then who are you people?"

"We've been trying to tell you," said Loretta.

"This is Miss Westminster, and we're the girls from Miss Westminster's Fine School for Girls of Elizabeth, New Jersey," said Fredonia.

"We're on our way to Little Indian," said Carla and Marla.

"We've been hired for the summer to put on a cabaret act," said Merridith.

"At Franco's Famous Italian Spaghetti Inn and Overnight Campground," added Augusta.

"You're singers and dancers?" asked Warden Wilhelmina.

"Some of the best," said Miss Westminster proudly.

"I'm only at my best when I'm chewing gum," said Loretta.

"Me too," added Fredonia.

"This is terrible," said Warden Wilhelmina. She bowed her head. "You see, I've spread the word to all the other prison wardens in the state that the Poughkeepsie Popular Prison for People was now the new home of Grannie Caster and Her All-Girl Gang!"

"Oh, I'm so sorry," said Miss Westminster.

"Yeah," echoed the girls.

"If there were any way that we could become Grannie Caster and Her All-Girl Gang," added Miss Westminster, "you could certainly count on us!"

"That's mighty nice of you," said Warden Wilhelmina. "I knew when I saw you people that you had class!" She thought for a minute. "Say, maybe there is a way that you can help me save face," she added.

"Name it!" said Fredonia.

"Of course!" said Miss Westminster. "Anything short of staying in prison for the rest of our natural lives! What did you have in mind?''

"Well, the act that we had booked for the *Prison Follies* tonight canceled on us," said Warden Wilhelmina. "I'll drop all charges if you'll take over!"

"What charges?" demanded Merridith.

"Never mind!" said Miss Westminster. "It's a deal! What do you want us to do?"

"Let's put on a show!" said Warden Wilhelmina. "But we must hurry. The *Follies* starts in ten minutes!"

"But we don't have any of our music with us!" said Merridith.

"Or our costumes!" said Carla and Marla.

"Or *my* chewing gum!" added Loretta.

"You'll just have to fake it," said Warden Wilhelmina. "We barely have time to make it to the Prison Theatre!"

Miss Westminster gasped. "I've never faked anything in my whole life," she said.

"There's always a first time, sister!" said Warden Wilhelmina.

Miss Westminster sighed.

The girls sighed.

With Warden Wilhelmina in the lead, they all rushed across the yard to the stage entrance of the Prison Theatre.

The Stage Manager said, "The show must go on!"

The girls took their places on stage. Miss Westminster sat down at the piano. Warden Wilhelmina stood in the wings.

The curtain rose.

The prison audience went wild. "Yea! Yea!" they cheered.

Miss Westminster began to play. *Ping! Ping! Ping!*

The girls began to sing. "How lovely it is to be here! How lovely it is to see you! Mrs. Bluebird sends her greetings! Mrs. Cardinal sings a cheery hello!"

"Yea! Yea!" cheered the prisoners.

"We're a hit!" said Merridith.

"Ah jus' knew we would be!" said Augusta.

"Us too," said Carla and Marla.

"I was just awful!" said Loretta. "It's because I'm not chewing gum!"

10

Miss Westminster stood up. "Thank you! Thank you!" she said, bowing to the audience.

"Yea! Yea!" cheered the prisoners.

"And now," continued Miss Westminster, "the girls will do a tap dance to my latest composition: 'When You Call, I'll Tap My Way Into Your Heart'!"

"Yea! Yea!" cheered the prisoners.

"Hit it, girls!" said Miss Westminster as she began playing the piano.

The girls began dancing. *Tap! Tap! Tap! Tap! Tap! Tap! Tap! Tap! Tap! Tap! Tap! Tap! Tap! Tap! Tap! Tap!*

Miss Westminster stopped playing.

The girls stopped dancing.

Miss Westminster took a bow.

The girls took a bow.

"Yea! Yea!" cheered the prisoners.

Miss Westminster and the girls headed offstage.

"Is that it?" cried Warden Wilhelmina.

"That's all we had time to prepare," said Fredonia.

"Yeah," said Merridith. "We were going to practice the other numbers after we got to Little Indian."

"I can't believe this," said Warden Wilhelmina.

"Now will you release us?" said Loretta.

Warden Wilhelmina thought for a moment. Miss Westminster and the girls held their breaths.

"Well, we always have request time," said Warden Wilhelmina. "I'm afraid the girls will be disappointed if you don't let them request something . . ."

"Well, I'm not quite sure . . ." began Miss Westminster.

But Warden Wilhelmina interrupted her. ". . . and the last time the ladies didn't get their request, we had a riot!"

"Oh, my goodness," said Augusta, "we jus' never have riots in Atlanta!"

"Well, I suppose . . ." said Miss Westminster.

"We usually allow one request," said Warden Wilhelmina, "and we always let Mama Rosa make it, since she's the oldest and most influential prisoner here at the Poughkeepsie Popular Prison for

People." She turned toward the audience. "Mama Rosa, where are you?"

"Here I am!" yelled Mama Rosa from the back of the auditorium.

"You get to make the request!" said Warden Wilhelmina. "Come on up and say hello to these nice folks!"

Mama Rosa rushed up to the stage and began hugging Miss Westminster and the girls. "You've done my heart good," she said, "and now if you'll grant me this one request, I'll be in your debt forever!"

"Certainly," said Miss Westminster.

"Certainly," said the girls.

"What do you want us to sing?" asked Miss Westminster.

"What do you want us to dance?" asked the girls.

"Sing?" exclaimed Mama Rosa. *"Dance?* I don't want you to sing and dance! I want you to find my baby boy!" She began to sob.

Warden Wilhelmina put her arms around Mama Rosa. "It's the same old request every time we have a group," she said.

"I don't understand," said Miss Westminster.

"Tell them the story, Mama Rosa," said Warden Wilhelmina.

"Well, it all started ten years ago," began Mama Rosa with a sob. "I was running this really classy Italian restaurant here in Poughkeepsie, but I wouldn't buy my spaghetti from the Pasta Nostra, so they ran me out of business. I had to turn to a life of crime in order to make a living. Naturally, I was captured and sent up for life!" Mama Rosa's voice cracked. Warden Wilhelmina put her arms around her again. "My only son, Giorgio, said he wouldn't rest until he paid my debt to society," continued Mama Rosa, "but I haven't heard from him since. I think he may have turned to a life of crime himself. I want you to find him for me!"

"Well, uh, sure," said Miss Westminster. She looked at the girls. "We'll do whatever we can, won't we, girls?"

"Yeah!" said the girls.

The prisoners cheered: "Yea! Yea!" Then they began filing out of the auditorium.

Mama Rosa hugged Miss Westminster and the girls again. "I have a good feeling about you," she said. "I just know you'll be

12

successful and find my baby boy for me!'' She turned to Warden Wilhelmina. "I never did have any faith in that rock 'n' roll group we had last year!'' she added.

"Well, now, if you'll just show us the way out, we'll be on our way,'' said Miss Westminster.

"What about our clothes?'' asked Augusta.

"What about Herman?'' asked Loretta.

"I'll have your civilian clothes sent over from your unused cells,'' said Warden Wilhelmina, "but who's Herman?''

"Herman is our bus driver,'' said Merridith.

"They took him to the Men's Prison,'' said Carla and Marla.

"Not to worry,'' said Warden Wilhelmina. She picked up a telephone and said, "Send out the prisoners' clothes and bus driver, and make it snappy!'' Then she turned to Miss Westminster and the girls. "Come on!'' she said.

Warden Wilhelmina showed Miss Westminster and the girls to the front of the prison.

Herman was standing by the prison bus. He had designer shopping bags in each hand. "Here are your street clothes,'' he said.

The Sheriff and his Grinning Deputies were standing at attention.

"Sorry for the inconvenience, ma'am,'' said the Sheriff to Miss Westminster. "It was just a case of mistaken identity.''

"No problem,'' said Miss Westminster. "We needed the practice anyway!''

The Sheriff looked puzzled.

Herman, Miss Westminster, and the girls climbed aboard the prison bus.

"I'll personally drive you back to where we arrested you,'' said the Sheriff.

"Okay,'' said Herman.

"Okay,'' said Miss Westminster and the girls.

"Don't forget Mama Rosa's request,'' said Warden Wilhelmina. She had out her blue lace handkerchief and was waving it.

"I won't!'' said Miss Westminster.

"We won't!'' said the girls.

"What's she talking about?'' asked Herman.

"You had to be there,'' said Miss Westminster.

When they arrived back at Aunt Millie's house, everyone got off

13

the prison bus and said good-bye to the Sheriff and the Grinning Deputies.

"That's strange," said Fredonia.

"What's strange?" asked Miss Westminster.

"The house looks just the way we left it," said Fredonia.

"Yeah," said Merridith, "the windows and doors are still all smashed in."

"And the front of the house is still leaning toward the street," added Loretta.

"Yeah," said Herman, "and it *still* doesn't look like anybody's home!"

"Of course Aunt Millie is at home," said Miss Westminster, "I'll just go up and knock!"

"No!" screamed Herman.

"No!" screamed the girls.

"Oh, don't worry," said Miss Westminster, "I'll just knock gently. You girls get on the bus and change your clothes. Herman, you keep an eye out for that Sheriff and his Grinning Deputies. I'm still not quite sure I trust that lot!"

"Okay, Miss Westminster," said Herman.

"Okay, Miss Westminster," said the girls.

Miss Westminster started toward the front porch.

"Is that you, Little Gertie?"

Miss Westminster looked up. A little old lady was running from the yard next door.

"Why it's Miss Higgenbothem!" said Miss Westminster. "Yes, yes, it's me, Little Gertie!"

Miss Higgenbothem looked at Miss Westminster's dress. "Did you just get out of prison?" she asked.

"It's a very long story, Miss Higgenbothem," said Miss Westminster. "Have you seen my Aunt Millie? I tried to, uh, rouse her earlier, but I didn't have too much luck."

"I noticed," said Miss Higgenbothem. She handed Miss Westminster a note. "Maybe this will explain why."

Miss Westminster took the note and read it. *"Aaaaagggggghhhhh!"* she screamed. Then she ran back to their bus.

CHAPTER THREE

Halfway Disappointment in Little Indian

"What's wrong, Miss Westminster?" asked Fredonia. Miss Westminster handed her the note. She read it to the girls:

Dear Little Gertie,
I'm sorry I wasn't here when you and your pupils arrived. I have decided to go to India on a pilgrimage. I'll be living in the Himalayas for several years. I met the cutest guru here in Poughkeepsie last week. He told me that I was the reincarnation of Marilyn Monroe!

Love,
Aunt Millie

"Well, what are we going to do *now?*" demanded Carla and Marla.

"I have decided that we will drive on to Little Indian tonight," declared Miss Westminster.

"None of this would ever have happened," said Merridith, "if we had done that in the first place, the way I said we should!"

"Don't be so self-righteous, Merridith," said Miss Westminster. "We all make mistakes."

"Ah never make mistakes," said Augusta.

"I don't drive very well at night, Miss Westminster," said Herman, "especially after I've been in prison all day."

"Don't worry, Herman," said Miss Westminster, "we'll all tell you where to go."

"That's what I was afraid of," muttered Herman.

Herman started the bus and pulled away from the curb with the tires squealing.

"Watch it, Herman!" shouted Miss Westminster. "I don't want to be arrested again."

"Actually, prison wasn't so bad," said Augusta.

Miss Westminster and the other girls groaned.

"I didn't get to buy any chewing gum while we were there," said Fredonia.

"Me either," said Loretta. "How can I possibly sing and dance if I'm not chewing gum?"

"Please, girls," said Miss Westminster. "At least we're free. Let's be thankful for small favors!"

"Did you say *flavors?*" asked Loretta. "I don't care what flavors I get, just as long as I get some gum!"

Miss Westminster hung her head and began sobbing quietly.

Soon they had left the bright lights of Poughkeepsie behind them, crossed the bridge over the Hudson River, and were headed toward the Catskill Mountains.

They slowed down for Kingston, whizzed past West Hurley, speeded through Glenford, zipped through Ashokan, left rubber in Shokan, and roared through Boiceville.

When they reached Mount Tremper, Herman said, "I'm having trouble seeing on these narrow mountain roads."

Miss Westminster and the girls all rushed to the front of the bus. "Just do what we tell you to do, Herman!" they all yelled.

"Don't crowd me, don't crowd me!" Herman shouted back as he gasped for air.

"Turn right here!" yelled Miss Westminster.

"Keep left!" yelled Fredonia as they careened around a steep mountain curve.

"You're over the center line!" shouted Merridith.

"Here comes another car!" screamed Augusta.

"Watch out for that rock slide!" shouted Carla and Marla.

"Hairpin curve straight ahead!" yelled Loretta.

"Shift into second!" screamed Miss Westminster.

"Shift into first!" shouted Fredonia.

"What does that red light mean?" yelled Augusta.

Herman looked at the dashboard. "We don't have any brakes!" he screamed. Then he slumped over the steering wheel in a faint.

"Somebody grab the steering wheel!" shouted Carla and Marla.

Miss Westminster pushed Herman out of the driver's seat and grabbed the steering wheel.

"What are those lights down there in the valley?" yelled Loretta.

"That must be Little Indian!" cried Miss Westminster.

"Look at the speedometer!" shouted Carla and Marla.

"Forty!" screamed Loretta.

"Fifty!" screamed Fredonia.

"Sixty!" screamed Augusta.

"Eighty!" screamed Merridith.

"One hundred!" screamed Carla and Marla.

"Good heavens!" cried Miss Westminster.

"Turn right!" shouted Loretta.

"One hundred and twenty!" cried Fredonia as the bus careened to the right on two wheels.

"Turn left!" shouted Loretta.

"One hundred and forty!" cried Augusta as the bus careened to the left on two wheels.

"Watch out for those trees!" cried Merridith.

"One hundred and sixty!" cried Fredonia.

"Watch out for those rocks!" cried Merridith.

"One hundred and eighty!" cried Carla and Marla.

"We've reached the bottom of the hill, girls!" shouted Miss Westminster.

"We must be in Little Indian!" cried Loretta. "I think those were buildings we just whizzed by!"

"Red light up ahead!" cried Merridith.

"Too late!" screamed Miss Westminster.

"We're slowing down!" cried Carla and Marla. "One hundred and sixty! One hundred and forty! One hundred and twenty! One hundred! Eighty! Sixty! Forty! Twenty! Ten! Nine! Eight! Seven! Six! Five! Four! Three! Two! One!"

The bus stopped.

Everybody looked out through the front windshield. The headlights lit up a sign: FRANCO'S FAMOUS ITALIAN SPAGHETTI INN AND OVERNIGHT CAMPGROUND.

"We're here!" screamed Carla and Marla.

"What time is it?" asked Miss Westminster.

Loretta looked at her watch. "It's one o'clock in the morning," she said.

"What do we do now?" asked Merridith.

"We sleep until nine o'clock," said Miss Westminster.

Fredonia looked at Herman. He was still lying unconscious in the aisle of the bus. "Do you think we should try to revive Herman?" she asked.

Miss Westminster thought for a minute. "No, just let him sleep," she said.

"Ah've jus' never spent the night in a bus before," said Augusta. "Not even in Georgia!"

But nobody heard her. Everyone was sound asleep.

The morning sun peeked over the dark green Catskill Mountains and into the black-and-yellow school bus.

Herman sat up and looked around. "Where am I?" he asked with a yawn. "I was having this terrible dream. The brakes went out on the bus, and it was out of control and . . ."

"That wasn't a dream," said Fredonia as she gave a big stretch.

Miss Westminster sat up. "What time is it?" she asked.

Fredonia looked at her watch. "It's almost nine o'clock."

"Wake up the other girls for me," said Miss Westminster. "We're supposed to meet Franco at nine."

"Everybody wake up!" screamed Fredonia.

"Good heavens, Fredonia," said Miss Westminster, "I could have done that!"

The other girls opened their eyes.

"Ah was dreaming Ah was back in Georgia," said Augusta. "Ah'm hungry!"

"Us too," said Carla and Marla.

"We'll eat after we talk to Franco," said Miss Westminster. "Now get up and comb your hair. I want us to look our best when we meet Franco. Don't forget what you learned in your First Impressions Manners Class. You learned that first impressions count!"

18

"Then don't you think you ought to change your clothes, Miss Westminster?" asked Loretta.

Miss Westminster looked down at the prison uniform she still had on. "Oh, my heavens, yes!" she said.

The girls stood up, tucked their T-shirts into their shorts, brushed their hair with their fingers, and lined up outside the bus.

After Miss Westminster had changed her dress, she and the girls passed in review for Herman. "Well, what do you think, Herman?" she said.

"I think I'm getting too old for this," said Herman.

"No, no," said Miss Westminster. "I mean, how do we look?"

"You look okay, I guess," said Herman. He yawned. "If you don't mind, I think I'll fix these brakes, then get back on the bus and go to sleep."

"You do that, Herman dear," said Miss Westminster. "You've had a very trying experience."

"What about me?" asked Loretta. "I've had a very trying experience too!"

"You'll survive, dear," said Miss Westminster. "Now come along, girls. Franco is expecting us."

Miss Westminster and the girls walked up to the front door of Franco's Famous Italian Spaghetti Inn and Overnight Campground and went inside.

The lobby was empty.

"This is strange," said Miss Westminster. "I wonder where all the guests are."

They walked over to the registration desk and Miss Westminster rang the bell.

A short, fat man appeared. "How many nights do you want to stay?" he asked. "I can give you very good rates!"

"I'm Miss Westminster," said Miss Westminster, "and these are the cabaret singers and dancers you hired for the summer!"

The girls all waved.

The short, fat man, who of course was Franco, turned pale. "Oh, my goodness," he said, "didn't you get my telegram?"

"What telegram?" said Miss Westminster.

"I've canceled the show!" said Franco.

"What?" screamed Miss Westminster.

19

"What?" screamed the girls.

"I had to," said Franco sorrowfully. "I haven't had any guests in months!"

"But . . . but . . . but . . ." said Miss Westminster.

"But . . . but . . . but . . ." said the girls.

"I'm sorry," said Franco. "I really am. But I do have a friend in Nome, Alaska, who's always looking for a class act!"

"Alaska!" cried Miss Westminster.

"Alaska!" cried the girls.

"Just let me think," said Miss Westminster. She sat down in a chair. Then she stood up. "Well, I guess we'll just have to get back on the bus and drive on to Nome. I don't know what else we can do."

"Oh, no," groaned the girls. "We're tired!"

"So am I," said Miss Westminster, "but . . ." She turned and looked at Franco. "Would it be possible for us to stay here just one night?"

Franco brightened and started counting, ". . . Five, six, seven . . . yes, yes, I can give you seven first-class rooms."

"Don't forget Herman," said Fredonia.

"Oh, yes," said Miss Westminster. "We'll need a room for our bus driver."

Franco's smile broadened. "I can give you eight first-class rooms for just over . . . let's see . . . one thousand dollars!"

Miss Westminster inhaled sharply. "I'm afraid we don't have that kind of money," she said weakly.

Franco stopped smiling. "Well, that's a different matter then," he said. He started dusting the top of the registration desk. "I'm afraid I can't help you!"

Miss Westminster looked disheartened.

The girls looked disheartened.

"We should have stayed in prison," said Loretta.

"What?" said Franco.

"Nothing," said Miss Westminster hurriedly. "Well, I guess we'll just have to sleep on the bus again, girls."

The girls groaned.

Franco softened. "Well, if you're *that* desperate, I guess you can stay here for free," he said, "but only for one night and only if you make up your own beds and cook your own meals. I had to let all the help go!"

"You've got a deal!" cried Miss Westminster. "Right, girls?"

"Right!" cried the girls.

"Come on," said Miss Westminster, "let's go tell Herman our change of plans!"

CHAPTER FOUR

Mad Mary Magillicuddy and Her Anti-Terrorist Squad

Miss Westminster and the girls hurried back to the bus.

Herman sat up and stretched. "What's wrong?" he asked.

"Franco canceled the show," said Miss Westminster.

"Oh, no!" said Herman.

"But he said we could spend the night here before we went on to Nome!" said Merridith.

"Nome?" said Herman. "Where's that?"

"Alaska!" said Miss Westminster.

"I wonder if they have chewing gum in Alaska," said Loretta.

"Alaska?" said Herman.

"Yeah," said Fredonia. "Franco has a friend up there who needs a class act too."

"Naturally, Franco thought of us," said Carla and Marla.

"Naturally," said Herman. He looked around the bus. "I doubt if this bus'll make it all the way to Alaska," he said.

"Sure it will," said Miss Westminster.

"Yeah," echoed the girls.

"But come on," said Miss Westminster, "we need to rest up before the big trip tomorrow."

"Wait a minute," said Herman. "Won't it cost a lot of money if we stay here at the inn?"

"Franco said we could stay free if we would clean up our mess," said Augusta.

"Well, all right," said Herman, "but I think this is all a big mistake."

Herman helped the girls and Miss Westminster with their bags.

Franco was standing at the front door of the inn, holding it open.

"Franco," said Miss Westminster, "this is Herman, our bus driver."

"Pleased to meet you," said Herman.

"The same to you," said Franco.

"Where do you want us to go?" asked Miss Westminster.

"You can have any empty room you can find," said Franco, "but you have to clean up your mess before you leave!"

"We shall!" shouted Herman, Miss Westminster, and the girls.

An hour later, everyone was all settled in and back down in the lobby with Franco.

"We haven't had any breakfast yet," said Miss Westminster.

"Help yourself to the kitchen," said Franco, "but just clean up your mess!"

"We shall!" shouted Herman, Miss Westminster, and the girls.

They all rushed to the kitchen and began opening the cupboards and the refrigerator.

"There's nothing in here but stuff for spaghetti dinners," said Fredonia.

"Ah jus' hardly ever eat spaghetti for breakfast in Atlanta," said Augusta.

"There's always a first time," said Herman.

"Well, come on, girls," said Miss Westminster, "let's get started."

Loretta boiled the water.

Merridith warmed the spaghetti sauce and meatballs.

Herman made the garlic toast.

Fredonia put the spaghetti into the boiling water.

Carla and Marla cut up tomatoes and lettuce for a salad.

Augusta mixed the oil and vinegar for the dressing.

Miss Westminster set the table.

When they had finished, they put all the food on the table and started eating.

They ate in silence for several minutes. Then Franco came into the dining room.

"I just talked to my friend in Nome," he said, "and he's ready to hire you in a minute!"

29

"I still don't think that bus of ours will make it all the way to Alaska," said Herman.

"Of course it will, Herman," said Miss Westminster. "You fixed the brakes, didn't you?"

"Yes," said Herman, "but . . ."

"Well, actually, the only way to get to my friend's place is by dogsled for the last five hundred miles," said Franco, "but it's a very popular place. There might even be some talent scouts from New York or Hollywood in the audience."

"Oh, really?" said Miss Westminster. She thought for a minute. "I wonder if we're ready for Nome?"

"I think we are," said Merridith. "We have a great show!"

"And we were a big hit while we were in prison," said Loretta.

"What?" said Franco.

"Nothing," said Miss Westminster. "When does your friend have to have an answer?"

"He'll give you an hour," said Franco. "After that, he's calling New York and Hollywood!"

"New York and Hollywood?" cried Augusta. "You mean he'd take us before somebody from New York or Hollywood? Oh, Miss Westminster, this is our big chance!"

"Well, I don't know, girls," said Miss Westminster.

"I'm still worried about that bus," said Herman.

"Let's go to Nome!" cried the girls.

"Well, let's practice first," said Miss Westminster, "and if I feel we're ready, then we'll go!"

"Yea!" cried the girls. They jumped up from the table and started for the stage in the ballroom.

"Clean up your mess!" shouted Franco.

They hurriedly cleaned up their mess. Then Franco, Herman, and Miss Westminster followed the girls into the darkened ballroom.

"Where are the spotlights?" asked Herman.

"On the left," said Franco.

"Help me with this piano first," said Miss Westminster.

Everybody helped move the piano to the right side of the stage.

Miss Westminster sat down at the piano. "We'll start with your number first, Fredonia," she said. "It needs the most work."

Fredonia frowned.

"*Hold it!*" shouted a deep voice from the rear of the darkened ballroom.

"Oh, oh," whispered Franco, "it's Mad Mary Magillicuddy, the High Sheriff of Minnewaska County. I wonder what she wants now? *What is it, Mad Mary?*" shouted Franco.

"*I want today's police cards!*" Mad Mary shouted back.

"*I don't have any* . . . Oh, oh," said Franco, "I forgot to have you people fill out the police cards when you registered," he whispered to Miss Westminster. "It's been so long since I had any guests."

"Police cards?" said Miss Westminster. "I thought they only did that in France!"

"Oh, no," said Franco. The sweat was beginning to pour from his brow. "We do it here in Minnewaska County too. It's part of Mad Mary's anti-terrorist campaign!"

"*The cards, Franco!*" shouted Mad Mary again.

"*Coming, Mad Mary!*" shouted Franco. "*We were just about to finish filling them out for you!*"

In the back of the darkened ballroom, Mad Mary stood silhouetted against the outside light. Several sets of eyes glowed on each side of her.

"Who's that with Mad Mary?" whispered Miss Westminster.

"That's her Anti-Terrorist Squad," Franco whispered back. "They strike terror into the hearts of everybody in Little Indian!"

"We can believe that!" said Carla and Marla.

"*They'll never take me alive!*" screamed Merridith.

"Keep quiet, Merridith!" hissed Miss Westminster.

When they all reached the rear of the ballroom, Mad Mary shouted, "*All right, I want you all up against the wall!*"

Everybody followed Franco and hurriedly lined up facing the wall, legs spread, hands spread, noses touching the cold plaster.

Mad Mary searched Miss Westminster and the girls.

The Anti-Terrorist Squad searched Franco and Herman.

"What are you looking for, Mad Mary?" asked Franco.

"Weapons!" said Mad Mary.

"Weapons?" said Miss Westminster. "What kind of weapons?"

"Machine guns, bazookas, plastic explosives, whatever you terrorists have been able to lay your hands on," said Mad Mary.

"We're not terrorists," said Fredonia.

"That's what they all say, sister," said Mad Mary. "All right, put your hands down and turn around slowly."

Franco, Herman, Miss Westminster, and the girls all turned around slowly and faced Mad Mary and her Anti-Terrorist Squad.

"I want to know where you hid the plastic explosives," said Mad Mary.

"We don't have any plastic explosives," said Loretta.

"Well, how do you make your bombs then?" demanded Mad Mary.

"What bombs?" asked Miss Westminster.

"Excuse me, Mad Mary," said Franco, "but this lady and her girls are from Elizabeth, New Jersey."

"A hotbed of terrorism if there ever was one!" said Mad Mary.

"No, no," said Miss Westminster. "I am the Headmistress of Miss Westminster's Fine School for Girls of Elizabeth, New Jersey! We do not teach terrorist tactics at our school!"

"We probably should," muttered Merridith. "I still wonder if I'm getting a quality education!"

Miss Westminster gave her a stony stare.

"Franco hired us to sing and dance for the summer," said Fredonia. "That's why we're here!"

"We're leaving for Nome in the morning," added Loretta.

"Well, all right," said Mad Mary, "but I'm going to keep an eye on you. I promised the good people of Minnewaska County that if they elected me sheriff I would rid this county once and for all of the terrorists, and I intend to do just that!"

"I think that's admirable, Mad Mary," said Miss Westminster.

"Us too," said Herman and the girls.

"Don't get smart with me, sisters . . ." said Mad Mary. She looked at Herman. ". . . and brother!"

"We weren't . . ." began Miss Westminster.

"All right, Franco," interrupted Mad Mary, "just give me the police cards and be quick about it! I'm in a hurry. I've got to round up those terrorists at the Little Indian Socialist Bookstore before I head on up to Albany!"

26

Franco frantically finished filling out the remaining police cards and handed them to Mad Mary. Mad Mary grabbed the cards, stuffed them into her shirt pocket, and then blew her police whistle. The Anti-Terrorist Squad stood at attention.

Mad Mary turned and began goose-stepping out of the inn, followed, in step, by the Anti-Terrorist Squad.

"Whew," said Franco, wiping his brow, "that was close!"

"Are there really terrorists in Little Indian?" asked Loretta.

"Mad Mary thinks there are," said Franco. "She is determined to prove to the New York Legislature that they should give her all the money she wants for anti-terrorist weapons."

"Good grief," said Miss Westminster. "That woman is dangerous!"

"You're telling me!" said Franco.

"I wonder if Mama Rosa's son could be one of the terrorists that Mad Mary is looking for," said Fredonia.

"Who's Mama Rosa?" asked Franco.

"She's the lady we met in prison," said Carla and Marla.

"What?" said Franco.

"Nothing," said Miss Westminster.

"Is she gone yet?"

Everybody looked up. A postman stood trembling in the doorway.

"Yes, Emmett, she's gone," said Franco. "Come on in."

Franco introduced the postman to Herman, Miss Westminster, and the girls.

"I didn't want Mad Mary to see me," said Emmett. "She didn't get any anti-terrorist weapons catalogs today and it makes her mad. She thinks I steal them from her."

"Got any mail for me, Emmett?" asked Franco.

"Just one letter," said Emmett. "It has a New York City postmark on it." He handed the letter to Franco.

Franco slit it open. "It's from the GAFIA," he said. "They want to hold their annual convention here in Little Indian, and they want to stay here!"

"What's the GAFIA?" asked Herman.

"The Gangsters And Finks International Association," said Franco. Then he gasped. "Good heavens! They'll be here tonight!

Listen to this: 'Sorry for the short notice, but we've just been given twenty-four hours to get out of town.' "

"That's wonderful!" cried Miss Westminster. "Now that you'll have guests, we won't have to go all the way to Nome to put on our cabaret act. We can stay right here in Little Indian!"

"Yea!" cried the girls.

But Franco had a worried look on his face.

CHAPTER FIVE

The GAFIA Makes an Offer

"Well, I guess this means I can head on back to Elizabeth for the summer," said Herman.

"Of course it does, Herman dear," said Miss Westminster.

"We'll miss you, Herman," said the girls.

"I'll miss you too," said Herman. He picked up his suitcase and headed for the door of the inn.

Miss Westminster waved her handkerchief. "See you in September, Herman dear!" she said.

"Okay," said Herman as he climbed onto the bus.

"Don't go back by way of Poughkeepsie!" shouted Fredonia.

But Herman already had the school bus squealing away from the curb in a cloud of smoke.

Miss Westminster looked at Franco. "What's wrong?" she asked. "You don't seem very excited."

"Would you be excited if there was a chance that your guests might try to steal your famous secret spaghetti sauce recipe?" cried Franco.

"I beg your pardon!" said Miss Westminster. "We are not thieves!"

"No!" cried the girls.

"I'm not talking about *you,*" said Franco, "I'm talking about the GAFIA, those gangsters and finks! You must promise me that you will never reveal my secret spaghetti sauce recipe to them!"

Miss Westminster laughed. "But Franco, we're singers and dancers," she said. "How could we ever be in a position to reveal your secret spaghetti sauce recipe?"

"Yeah," said the girls.

"Uh, well, that's what I have to talk to you about," said Franco. "You see, when I wasn't getting any guests, I had to fire all my help, remember? I'm going to need some maids and cooks and . . . I can't afford to hire anybody else until the GAFIA pays its bill, so . . ."

"You mean you want *me* to work as a maid?" cried Merridith.

"Ah've jus' never been a cook before," said Augusta.

"Us either!" said Carla and Marla.

"It's just temporary," said Franco, "until *I* get paid! Besides, that's the only way you'll get to put on your cabaret act!"

"This is blackmail!" cried Loretta.

Franco shrugged.

Miss Westminster screwed up her mouth. "Well, if that's the way it is, then that's the way it is."

"I knew you'd understand," said Franco. "Now then, we've got a lot to do, because the GAFIA will be here this evening, all five hundred of them!"

"Five hundred?" cried Miss Westminster.

"Five hundred?" cried the girls.

"I wonder if this is the way all Broadway stars get their start," said Loretta.

"Ah certainly hope so," said Augusta.

With Franco directing, Miss Westminster and the girls cleaned up all the rooms and changed all the sheets.

During the afternoon, Miss Westminster rolled up 5,000 meatballs and made 250 gallons of spaghetti sauce, using Franco's famous secret recipe.

The girls polished all the silver and folded 1,000 napkins.

By evening, the first members of the GAFIA began arriving. Some came in black limousines, some came in campers.

A man dressed in a black leisure suit jumped out of the first limousine. He rushed up to Franco, Miss Westminster, and the girls. They were all standing in front of the inn, lined up to greet the new arrivals.

"I'm Sammy Smith," said the man. "I'm the President of the GAFIA. I'm here to see that all the protection is in force, you know what I mean?"

"What protection?" asked Franco.

"We'll need armed guards outside each room where a GAFIA member is staying or, in the case of some of our poorer GAFIA members, outside the campers. Then, inside the inn, we'll need armed guards on the stairs and at the front, side, and back entrances."

Franco pointed to Miss Westminster and the girls. "I'm still in the process of issuing them their weapons," he said, "but never fear, we'll be ready!"

Miss Westminster and the girls looked stunned.

Sammy said, "They look tough enough, especially the old bat there! You've done a swell job here!"

Miss Westminster gasped and clutched at her throat.

"Thanks," said Franco.

Twenty black limousines had now pulled up in front of the inn. Men were jumping out of all of them. They all had on black pants, black jackets with vests, and white spats on their black tennis shoes. They were all smoking cigars.

"I hate cigars," said Miss Westminster. "They make me deathly ill!" She started coughing.

The girls started coughing.

The GAFIA members began piling their suitcases onto the curb.

Franco took a bell out of his pocket and rang it. "Bellhops!" he yelled. Then he looked at Miss Westminster and the girls.

Miss Westminster and the girls hurried to the curbside, picked up all the luggage, and carried it inside the inn.

The members of the GAFIA began lining up at the registration desk.

"Don't forget to have them fill out the police cards for Mad Mary!" yelled Fredonia.

"Police?" screamed all the GAFIA members.

"Uh, well, yes. Our sheriff, Mad Mary Magillicuddy, uh, kind of likes to know who's, uh, in town," said Franco. "It's, uh, kind of like the law here."

"Well, we certainly wouldn't want to break the law, would we, fellows?" said Sammy Smith, winking.

All the other GAFIA members winked back. Then they began filling out the police cards.

Franco was hurriedly calculating the room rates. He had a smile on his face. "That'll be ten thousand dollars for all of you," he said to Sammy Smith. "Would you care to make a good-faith deposit?"

Sammy Smith smiled. "I'd sort of like to make you an offer," he said.

Franco gulped. "What did you have in mind?" he asked.

"We sort of thought five hundred dollars would cover everything," said Sammy. "You know, a dollar for each GAFIA member. That's usually our top offer."

Franco swallowed hard. "Whatever you say, sir," he said. "Perhaps I *have* overpriced the rooms."

"We appreciate your being so accommodating," said Sammy.

"Not at all," said Franco. He was perspiring heavily.

Finally, all 500 GAFIA members had registered. Those who were staying in the inn had been shown to their rooms. Those who were staying in their campers had been plugged in and turned on.

Miss Westminster and the girls collapsed in the lobby.

"I'm exhausted," said Fredonia.

"Us too," echoed the rest of the girls.

"Ah've never worked so hard in all my life," said Augusta.

"I think I'm going to bed," said Miss Westminster.

"Showtime!"

Everybody looked up. Franco was standing there grinning.

"What do you mean, 'showtime'?" said Fredonia.

"I told Sammy Smith all about your cabaret act," said Franco, "and he's just thrilled to death. In fact, all five hundred members of the GAFIA will be in the ballroom tonight at eight o'clock to catch it!"

"Tonight?" gasped Miss Westminster.

"Tonight?" gasped the girls.

"Tonight!" said Franco; then he disappeared.

Miss Westminster looked at her watch. "We have exactly one hour to get ready for this performance," she said weakly.

The girls groaned.

Then Miss Westminster squared her shoulders. "Oh, I know you're tired, girls," she said, "but we have to remember that this is our big chance!"

"She's right," said Merridith.

"That's easy for *you* to say," said Loretta. "You're not chewing-gum-dependent like me and Fredonia."

"Yeah," said Fredonia.

"The show must go on," said Miss Westminster.

"Yeah," said Carla and Marla, "but does it have to go on *tonight?*"

"Tonight and every night," said Miss Westminster, "until we get it right. Then we'll be ready for Broadway!"

"Or even Atlanta!" added Augusta.

They all headed down the deserted corridor toward the ballroom. Miss Westminster opened the door and out popped Franco in a huge cloud of black smoke.

"There you are!" said Franco.

"What's going on here?" demanded Fredonia. "Where's all this smoke coming from?"

"Oh, it's just the smoke from the GAFIA's cigars," said Franco.

"The GAFIA?" said Miss Westminster. "But it's not eight o'clock yet!"

"I know," said Franco. He smiled through the haze. "They just couldn't wait. All five hundred members of the GAFIA are already here!"

"But we're not ready!" shouted Miss Westminster.

"No!" echoed the girls.

"But the GAFIA's ready," said Franco, "and when the GAFIA's ready, everybody's ready!"

Miss Westminster and the girls formed a human chain and Franco led them through the thick smoke onto the stage.

The members of the GAFIA began whistling and cheering. The noise was deafening.

Franco helped Miss Westminster move the piano to the right side of the stage.

The GAFIA cheered and whistled.

The girls took their places center stage.

The GAFIA cheered and whistled.

"I can't see you, girls," shouted Miss Westminster, "but we'll do the ensemble tap dance first!"

"Okay, Miss Westminster!" shouted the girls. They lined up, shoulder to shoulder, hands around one another's waists.

33

"Are you ready, girls?" shouted Miss Westminster.

"Ready!" shouted the girls.

Ping! Ping! Ping! went Miss Westminster on the piano.

Tap! Tap! Tap! began the girls.

The members of the GAFIA came to their feet in a standing ovation. The cheers shook the ballroom.

Pong! Pong! Pong! continued Miss Westminster.

Tap! Tap! Tap! continued the girls.

Franco turned a spotlight on Fredonia. Fredonia tapped a circle around the rest of the girls.

The GAFIA members stood up again and cheered.

Ping! Pong! Ping! continued Miss Westminster.

Tap! Tap! Tap! continued the girls. Then they all fell to the floor in splits.

The GAFIA members cheered wildly and shouted for more.

When the applause had subsided, Miss Westminster said, "Our next number will be one of my original compositions!"

The members of the GAFIA stood up and cheered.

Ping! Ping! Pong! Pong! began Miss Westminster.

"How lovely it is to be here!" sang the girls. "How lovely it is to see you! Mrs. Bluebird sends her greetings! Mrs. Cardinal sings a cheery hello!"

"Yea!" cried the members of the GAFIA. "Yea! Yea! Yea!"

Miss Westminster stood up from the piano.

The girls bowed.

"Pull down the curtain, Franco!" shouted Miss Westminster.

Franco lowered the curtain.

"I can't breathe!" wheezed Fredonia.

"Us either," wheezed Carla and Marla.

"I was just awful," said Loretta, "and I'm sure *everybody* knows why!"

"Ah jus' simply had no idea that show business would be like this," said Augusta.

"You and me both," said Merridith.

"I don't think I'll ever recover from this," said Miss Westminster.

"Well, you'll have to," said Franco, "because the GAFIA wants its banquet served right away!"

CHAPTER SIX

Mr. Spaghetti Man

"I think we need to renegotiate our contract," said Fredonia.

"What contract?" said Franco.

"Never mind!" said Miss Westminster. She sighed. "What do you want us to do?"

"Follow me," said Franco.

Miss Westminster and the girls followed Franco through the smoke-filled ballroom to the kitchen.

Miss Westminster quickly put on an apron and a chef's hat and began cooking the 5,000 meatballs.

Fredonia poured Franco's secret spaghetti sauce into 100 saucepans and began warming them.

Carla and Marla began buttering 1,000 pieces of Italian bread with garlic butter.

Merridith began chopping up 250 tomatoes and 100 heads of lettuce.

Loretta began cooking 100 pots of spaghetti.

Augusta began mixing fifty bottles of oil and fifty bottles of vinegar.

Finally, the banquet was ready.

Franco called everybody together. "If any member of the GAFIA asks you for my secret spaghetti sauce recipe, take down his name," he said, "and I'll let Mad Mary deal with him. That recipe is the reason for the fame and fortune of Franco's Famous Italian Spaghetti Inn and Overnight Campground and nobody's going to get it!"

"Okay, Franco," said Miss Westminster.

"Okay, Franco," said the girls.

With Franco in the lead, Miss Westminster and the girls began pushing the carts of food toward the ballroom.

When they reached the ballroom, Franco opened the doors and out rushed more billowing clouds of black smoke.

Franco hurriedly closed the doors. "It's worse than ever," he said. "What are we going to do?"

Miss Westminster thought. Then she said, "Remember our Fire Manners Class, girls? We'll use what we learned in that class to help us serve the banquet!"

"What did we learn?" asked Loretta.

Miss Westminster raised an eyebrow and inhaled sharply. "We learned," she said, "that whenever there is a lot of smoke in the room where you are serving a meal, it is considered perfectly proper to get down on the floor and hand the food *up* to the table!"

"I thought you were supposed to get out of a building if there was a lot of smoke," said Franco.

Miss Westminster looked at him with arched eyebrows. "It depends on your breeding!" she said.

"Yeah!" said the girls.

Franco looked chastised.

Miss Westminster and the girls put all the serving carts in a long row and then crouched down on the floor behind each one and began pushing them slowly toward the doors of the ballroom.

Franco opened the doors again. The smoke began billowing out in great black clouds.

With Miss Westminster in the lead, the girls began crawling on their hands and knees, pushing the carts in front of them.

'The air *is* a little fresher down here, isn't it?" said Fredonia with a grunt.

"That's what we learned in our Fire Manners Class," grunted Miss Westminster.

Miss Westminster pushed her cart to the first table, then began handing plates of spaghetti *up* to the table. The GAFIA members didn't seem to notice the hands with plates of spaghetti in them coming from the floor.

When she finished serving the first table, Miss Westminster pushed her serving cart to the next table.

Fredonia arrived at the first table and began reaching *up* to put the spaghetti sauce on top of the spaghetti. She missed a few plates, but the GAFIA members didn't seem to notice the sauce all over their spats.

Loretta's cart of meatballs bumped into Fredonia's cart of spaghetti sauce, spilling some of the sauce and some of the meatballs onto the floor.

"Watch it!" shouted Fredonia.

"I'm sorry," said Loretta, "but I can't see anything in this fog!"

"You're telling me," said Fredonia.

"I have an idea," said Loretta. "Let's get under the table and try serving from there."

"Okay," said Fredonia. "Maybe it'll be a little easier to breathe."

Just as they started to crawl under the table, four other carts bumped into them. When they turned around, Carla was covered with vinegar and Marla was covered with oil. Augusta and Merridith were covered with lettuce and tomatoes. Garlic bread was all over the floor.

Fredonia and Loretta helped the other girls clean up the mess, and then they all got under the first table.

"Ah simply have to rest," said Augusta as she began curling up in a corner.

"Us too," said the rest of the girls.

". . . that somewhere here in Little Indian is a mysterious Mr. Spaghetti Man who has the ability to destroy or revolutionize the spaghetti industry and . . ."

"I think I'm going to . . ." Loretta started to say, but Fredonia said, "Sh-h-h!"

"What's the matter?" asked Merridith.

"I want to hear what the GAFIA members are saying," said Fredonia.

The girls all listened.

". . . but how do we know this here Mr. Spaghetti Man will come across and accept our offer? . . ."

"What are they talking about?" said Merridith.

"Sh-h-h!" said Fredonia. "Listen!"

". . . he'll come across, and when he does, anybody who wants

37

spaghetti will have to come to us! We'll control all the spaghetti in the world . . .''

All the GAFIA members started laughing an evil laugh. "Ha-ha-ha-ha-ha-ha-ha-ha-ha-ha!"

"Who's this Mr. Spaghetti Man they're talking about?" whispered Carla and Marla.

Fredonia thought for a minute. Then she gasped. "It has to be Franco!" she said. "He's famous around these parts for his spaghetti!"

"Of course!" said Loretta. "And the GAFIA is out to get him!"

"Ah jus' love spaghetti," said Augusta, "even if it isn't southern!"

"I do too," said Merridith.

"Us too," said Carla and Marla.

"Me too," said Fredonia, "but it looks as if the only way we'll be able to get any is to buy it from the . . . Sh-h-h! . . . Listen!"

". . . we'll be able to sell it cheap and put all the other spaghetti people out of business, and then we'll be able to charge any price we want! Ha-ha-ha-ha-ha-ha-ha-ha-ha-ha-ha-ha-ha-ha-ha-ha!"

"And Franco thought they only wanted to steal his secret spaghetti sauce recipe," said Fredonia. "He had no idea how really serious the situation is! This could affect the whole world!"

"This is terrible," said Loretta. "I'm going to give those people a piece of my mind!" She started to crawl out from under the table.

But Merridith stopped her. "You can't do that," she said. "We're not supposed to be hearing this. If the GAFIA finds out that we know what they're planning to do, why they'll . . . they'll . . . *never take me alive!*"

"Well, what are we going to do?" asked Loretta.

"We've got to get out of here fast," said Merridith, "while there's still time!"

"Let's hurry!" said Carla and Marla.

"But we haven't even served one table yet," said Augusta.

"I have an idea," said Fredonia. "You guys crawl toward the exit. I'm going up on the stage and make an announcement."

"Oh, be careful, Fredonia," said Loretta.

"Don't worry," said Fredonia. She paused. "You guys be careful too," she added.

Fredonia started crawling toward the stage.

The other girls started crawling toward the doors to the ballroom.

When Fredonia finally reached the stage, she bumped into Miss Westminster's cart.

"Oh, there you are," said Miss Westminster with a wheeze. "I've just finished serving all the spaghetti. How are you girls doing with the rest of the food?"

"Uh, well, it's a long and very dangerous story, Miss Westminster," said Fredonia, "but we think we can solve the problem. First of all, I'm going to make an announcement that the rest of the banquet will be served buffet style. We'll leave the carts together at one end of the room and let the GAFIA members serve themselves."

"That's a super idea," said Miss Westminster, "but what is this dangerous story you're talking about?"

"I'll tell you later," said Fredonia. "Why don't you hurry up and crawl back to the exit? You'll be safer that way. That's where the other girls are!"

"Well, okay, if you say so," said Miss Westminster, "but I certainly would like to know what's going on!"

"It's better if you don't know any more than you absolutely have to know," said Fredonia, "just in case you're captured and they try to make you talk!"

"Oh, my goodness," said Miss Westminster. She got back down on her hands and knees and started crawling hurriedly toward the exit.

Fredonia crawled up onto the stage. When she reached the microphone, she took a deep breath and stood up. "May I . . . *cough!* *cough!* . . . have your attention . . . *wheeze!* . . . *wheeze!* . . . please? We've decided . . . *cough!* . . . *cough!* . . . to serve the rest of the banquet . . . *wheeze!* . . . *wheeze!* . . . buffet style! Dig in . . . *cough!* . . . *cough!* . . . *wheeze!* . . . *wheeze!*" Then she fell to the floor. She could hear the sound of thundering hooves as the GAFIA members dashed to the food carts and filled their plates with spaghetti sauce, meatballs, salad, and garlic toast.

When the GAFIA members were finally seated again, Fredonia crawled off the stage and headed for the doors to the ballroom.

Franco, Miss Westminster, and the rest of the girls were waiting for her.

"That was a good idea, serving the banquet buffet style," said Franco. "I'm sure that when you first started to serve the tables, the GAFIA members at each table asked you about my secret spaghetti sauce recipe, didn't they? It must have been terrible!"

"It was terrible all right," said Fredonia, "but it's not just your secret spaghetti sauce recipe they want!" She looked at the other girls. "Have you said anything about it?" she asked.

"No," said Loretta, "we were too scared. It's so horrible!"

"Yeah!" said Carla and Marla.

"It's jus' awful," said Augusta. "Ah jus' can't believe it!"

"What could be more terrible than somebody wanting to steal the secret recipe for my famous spaghetti sauce?" demanded Franco.

"Well, while we were sitting under one of the tables," said Fredonia, "we overheard something else the GAFIA is planning to do!"

"*Under* one of the tables?" said Miss Westminster.

"It's a long story," said Merridith.

"Tell me anyway," said Miss Westminster.

"Well, as I said," continued Fredonia, "we were sitting under this table and we heard the GAFIA members talking about controlling the whole spaghetti industry!"

"That's terrible," said Miss Westminster. "Just how do they plan to do it?"

"They're going to make Franco some kind of offer and force him to join up with them!" said Fredonia.

Franco turned pale.

Miss Westminster looked at him. "Did they mention Franco by name?" she said.

"No," said Loretta, "they called him Mr. Spaghetti Man!"

"It was awful!" said Carla and Marla.

"*Mr. Spaghetti Man?*" said Miss Westminster. "Well, how do you know they were talking about Franco?"

"Who else would they be talking about?" said Augusta.

"She's right," said Franco. "What am I going to do?"

Miss Westminster thought for a minute. "We must pretend that

40

we don't know anything about this," she said. "That may be the only way we can save our lives!"

"You mean, business as usual?" said Franco.

"Exactly," said Miss Westminster.

"Well, then," said Franco, "you girls have to get ready for the two A.M. show!"

"The *what?*" screamed Miss Westminster.

"The *what?*" screamed the girls.

"Oh—did I forget to tell you that the GAFIA always demands a two A.M. cabaret at their conventions?" said Franco.

Miss Westminster and the girls fell to the floor.

"Just let me know if you need anything else," said Franco. "I have to go somewhere and think." He slowly headed down the corridor.

CHAPTER SEVEN

The Saintly Survivalist Sect Sets up Camp

Ring! Ring! Ring! Ring! Ring!
Miss Westminster opened one eye.
"What's that?" said Fredonia.
Ring! Ring! Ring! Ring! Ring!
"It's the telephone," said Miss Westminster. She opened the other eye and picked up the receiver. "Hello!"
"The GAFIA wants its breakfast," said Franco.
"What time is it?" asked Miss Westminster.
"It's six A.M.," said Franco.
"Good heavens," said Miss Westminster. "We were up until four A.M. singing and dancing for them. How could they possibly be hungry two hours later?"
"You know the GAFIA," said Franco. "Anything is possible!"
"You're telling me," muttered Miss Westminster. "Oh, all right," she said, "I'll get the girls up and we'll be down in a few minutes."
"Stop by my office first," said Franco. "I have some news for you."
Miss Westminster hurried the girls out of bed, got them dressed, then rushed them downstairs to Franco's office.
Franco was sitting behind his desk holding an envelope.
"What's the news?" asked Miss Westminster.
"I hope it's *good* news," said Fredonia.
"Yeah," said Loretta, "we could sure use some *good* news."
"Yeah!" echoed the rest of the girls.

42

"I have here in my hand," said Franco, "a letter from the President of the Saintly Survivalist Sect in Forty Trees, Idaho. He wants to hold the national convention of his organization here at Franco's Famous Italian Spaghetti Inn and Overnight Campground!"

"What does that have to do with us?" demanded Merridith.

"Don't you see?" said Franco.

"I'm afraid not," said Loretta with a yawn.

"Us either," said Carla and Marla.

Franco sighed. "They're probably after my secret spaghetti sauce recipe too," he said. "And whatever else they can get out of me. It's a conspiracy!"

"Oh," said Miss Westminster, "now I see!"

"You want us to be on the alert," said Augusta, "is that it?"

"Of course it is," said Franco. "Five hundred members of the Saintly Survivalist Sect will be arriving here tonight!"

"*What?*" screamed Miss Westminster.

"*What?*" screamed the girls.

"Of course," continued Franco, "that part of it isn't so bad. It means that much more money for the inn."

"Will this inn hold a thousand people?" asked Merridith.

"Well, we'll probably have to put some beds in the closets and in the bathrooms," said Franco, "but you'll manage."

"*We'll* manage?" cried Miss Westminster.

"Do you expect us to take care of a thousand people by ourselves?" demanded Fredonia.

"Remember our agreement," said Franco.

"Don't you think it's time you hired a regular staff?" asked Augusta.

"Oh, I'd really like to," said Franco, "I really would, but I haven't received any money from the GAFIA yet. No, I'm afraid that we'll just have to stick to our original agreement. It's just that you'll have to do double duty!"

"Triple!" said Loretta.

"Quadruple!" said Fredonia.

"What comes after that?" asked Carla and Marla.

"Ah do more than anybody else does," complained Augusta. "Jus' look at these beautiful hands!"

Outside Franco's office window, horns had begun to honk.

"They're early!" said Franco. "Come on!"

"What about the GAFIA's breakfast?" said Miss Westminster.

"They'll just have to eat banquet leftovers," said Franco.

Franco, Miss Westminster, and the girls rushed to the lobby.

Several RVs, campers, and pickup trucks pulling house trailers had parked in front of the inn. They were lined up as far down Little Indian's main street as the eye could see.

The honking continued. It was deafening.

The driver of the lead RV got out and walked into the lobby where Franco, Miss Westminster, and the girls were standing. He was tall and was dressed in a Special Air Service Regiment Smock and blue jeans. He was wearing Wellington boots. Around his neck he had a pair of Brunton Rubber Armored 8 × 30 binoculars, a Brunton Model 8040 compass, and a long green flashlight. In his left hand he carried a crossbow.

"You Franco?" he said to Miss Westminster.

Miss Westminster blinked; then she pointed to Franco.

Franco stuck out his hand. "Welcome to Franco's Famous Italian Spaghetti Inn and Overnight Campground," he said.

"I'm Luger Colt," said the man, "and I'm President of the Saintly Survivalist Sect, better known as the SSS."

"Our home is your home," said Franco.

"We'll make it that way," said Luger with a grin.

The honking continued.

"I'm checking everybody in," added Luger.

"Come on then," said Franco, "and we'll fill out the necessary registration forms."

"Don't forget Mad Mary's police forms," said Loretta.

"Police?" said Luger. "You got police here?"

"It's just a little formality," said Franco. He gave Loretta a dirty look.

"You got any other people staying here?" asked Luger.

"There are five hundred members of the GAFIA," said Fredonia. "They arrived last night."

Luger snarled. "Those creeps!" he said. "I bet they're after the same thing we are!" Franco inhaled sharply. Luger looked at him. Then he turned to Miss Westminster and the girls. "Who are you people?" he asked.

44

"We're singers and dancers," said Miss Westminster. "We're headed for Broadway!"

"I'm just awful," said Loretta. "Would you like to know why?"

Luger wrinkled his nose. "What I'd like to know is who's going to unload our supplies," he said.

Franco looked at Miss Westminster and the girls. "They also do that," he said hurriedly.

Luger snapped his fingers. "Follow me then," he said.

Miss Westminster and the girls followed Luger outside and then began fanning out through the caravan of honking RVs, campers, and pickup trucks. Luger snapped his fingers again and all the members of the Saintly Survivalist Sect began getting out of their vehicles.

"Take these!" shouted a survivalist dressed in a coonskin cap and leather pants. He handed Miss Westminster ten Swedish Kombin knives and twenty-five Target Magnum revolvers.

"What do you want me to do with all this?" asked Miss Westminster.

"Just take care of them for me, baby," said the survivalist. "Oh, if you have the time, you might oil them a little!"

Miss Westminster looked up as Fredonia passed by carrying ten machine guns on her back. "Good heavens," she muttered, "what have I done to these sweet, darling girls?"

Carla and Marla passed by carrying two large wooden boxes each.

"What do you have in the boxes, girls?" asked Miss Westminster.

"Bullets," said Carla and Marla.

Augusta joined them with five rifles.

Loretta came up carrying two boxes of dynamite.

"We could start a war," said Carla and Marla.

"That's exactly what I'm afraid of," said Miss Westminster.

Merridith arrived with several bulletproof vests. "Boy, these people are really serious about getting Franco's secret spaghetti sauce recipe, aren't they?" she said.

Miss Westminster began wringing her hands. "It certainly looks that way," she said.

Finally, all 500 members of the SSS had been unloaded and

registered and had begun setting up their headquarters. Several campfires had been started both inside and outside the inn.

Miss Westminster and the girls, at Franco's request, began opening all the windows in the inn, which only increased the size of the campfires. They had just finished opening the last of the windows when Luger Colt appeared again.

"I'm calling a meeting," said Luger. "A serious matter has to be taken care of right away!"

Franco gulped. "Oh," he said, "is there anything wrong?"

"I want a green line!" said Luger.

"What's a green line?" asked Miss Westminster.

"If you had been in as many wars as I have," said Luger, "you'd know these things."

"I'm sorry," said Miss Westminster.

"We're sorry," said the girls.

Luger looked at Franco.

"I'm sorry too," said Franco.

"I want you to set up a boundary inside this inn and outside on the campground that the GAFIA cannot cross," said Luger, "and I want you to do it immediately! We don't want those creeps messing up our plans!"

"But the GAFIA members are guests of the inn too," said Miss Westminster.

"Yeah," said Fredonia, "they gave us a standing ovation last night!"

"They recognize talent when they see it," said Loretta, "even if I wasn't chewing gum."

"It doesn't matter," said Luger. "If one of those creeps crosses into our territory, we'll have to declare war!"

"You'll never take me alive!" screamed Merridith.

"Oh, my goodness," said Miss Westminster.

"I knew it," said Fredonia.

"And we'll be put in prison again," said Loretta, "this time for gunrunning!"

"What?" said Franco.

"Nothing!" said Miss Westminster.

"It's all my fault," said Franco. "If my secret spaghetti sauce wasn't so good . . ."

46

"What?" said Luger.

"Nothing," said Miss Westminster. "All right. We have a policy in this inn of administering to the needs of our guests. So if you want us to draw boundary lines here in this inn and on the campground, then we'll do it."

"I knew you'd see it my way," said Luger.

Miss Westminster turned to Franco. "Go get some green paint, Franco," she said. "We may as well get started."

Franco hurried away to his office. When he returned, he had seven cans of green paint and seven brushes. He also had seven maps of the inn and the campground. "I've indicated on these maps where the GAFIA and the SSS are staying," he said. "Make sure you paint the green lines in the right places!"

Miss Westminster and the girls each took a paintbrush, a can of paint, and a map and began painting green lines.

Miss Westminster painted a green line in the lobby and on the stairs.

Merridith painted a green line down the middle of each corridor.

Carla and Marla painted green lines in the bathrooms.

Augusta painted a green line in the kitchen and in the ballroom.

Fredonia painted green lines on the lawn, but they didn't show up too well.

Loretta painted green lines on the trees and shrubs, but they didn't show up too well either.

Finally, the boundaries had been painted and everybody had met back in Franco's office. Sammy Smith and Luger Colt were sitting on a white couch with a green stripe painted down the middle.

"Well, we're through," said Miss Westminster.

The girls sat down on the rug. They were all covered with green paint.

"Maybe not," said Franco.

"What do you mean?" asked Fredonia.

"Our guests have another request," said Franco.

Luger and Sammy stood up.

"We have decided that a green line just isn't good enough," said Luger.

"No," said Sammy.

"Well, what else did you have in mind?" asked Miss Westminster.

"We have to lay a few land mines," said Luger.

"Land mines!" said Loretta.

"And we also have to set up a few machine-gun nests," added Sammy.

"Machine-gun nests!" said Merridith.

"Good heavens!" said Miss Westminster.

"We'll all be killed!" said Carla and Marla.

"Oh, don't worry," said Luger. "We'll issue secret maps to you and the girls and Franco showing the locations." He pointed to Sammy. "It's these creeps who had better watch out!"

Sammy stuck out his tongue.

Franco divided up the girls.

Fredonia, Loretta, and Merridith went with Sammy to set up the machine-gun nests.

Carla, Marla, and Augusta went with Luger to lay the land mines.

Miss Westminster sat down on the white couch with the green stripe and began sobbing. "What have I done to all these wonderful, wonderful girls?" she said.

In an hour, the girls were all back with their secret maps. Fredonia handed them to Miss Westminster, who was still sobbing.

"It'll be all right, Miss Westminster," said Loretta soothingly. "If we're careful, maybe we won't get blown up into little bitty pieces!"

Miss Westminster began sobbing even more.

The girls all gathered around.

Finally, Miss Westminster had her sobbing under control. "Franco," she said, "we need to have a very serious talk. Things are getting rather dangerous around here. I'm worried about the girls' safety. I don't think our school insurance covers students injured in a war!"

"You think you have worries?" said Franco. "What about me and my secret spaghetti sauce recipe? At least nobody's planning to steal one of your *girls!*"

"I know, Franco," said Miss Westminster, "but I'm responsible for their minds *and* their bodies!"

"Well, what more could you ask for?" said Franco. "You can

cross the green lines any time you want to, and you have secret maps showing where all the land mines are buried and where the machine-gun nests are hidden. I mean, what else do you want?''

"Oh, I know, I know," said Miss Westminster. "I'm probably asking for too much, but . . ."

"You most certainly are," said Franco. "I bring you people up here so you can gain some experience for Broadway and just because you're exposed to a little danger, you start to back out on me!''

"Oh, no, no," said Miss Westminster hurriedly, "we're not backing out on you. We wouldn't do that, would we, girls?''

"Oh, no, no," said the girls.

"Well, I should certainly hope not," said Franco, "after all I've done for you!''

"And we're grateful for that too," said Miss Westminster.

"Yeah!" cried the girls.

"Well, then, I guess it's all settled," said Franco. He looked at Miss Westminster. "Well?''

Miss Westminster said, "Well, Franco, it's just that we all know that both the GAFIA and the SSS are after you and your secret spaghetti sauce recipe and whatever else they have in mind, and this has put the girls and me under a terrible strain, not knowing when the attack will come. We're too nervous even to practice our cabaret act!''

"Yeah!" said the girls.

"I have decided that we're not even going to think about getting to Broadway until this matter is settled," said Miss Westminster.

"Yeah!" said the girls.

"Oh, really?" said Franco. "That's too bad."

"But I do think that I have arrived at a possible solution to the problem," said Miss Westminster.

Franco and the girls drew closer to Miss Westminster.

"What is it?" Franco whispered.

CHAPTER EIGHT

Peace at Any Cost . . . Almost

"A high-level international conference," said Miss Westminster.

Franco thought for a minute. "Hmm," he said. "Exactly what did you have in mind?"

"You know," continued Miss Westminster, "a conference just like the ones they're always having in Geneva, Switzerland. I'm going to telephone both Luger Colt and Sammy Smith right now and tell them that we have to talk to them."

"Well, it might work," said Franco.

Miss Westminster picked up the telephone. She dialed Luger Colt's number. "Be in the ballroom in ten minutes!" she said. Then she hung up. Then she dialed Sammy Smith's number. "Be in the ballroom in ten minutes," she said. Then she hung up again.

"You're a born diplomat," said Franco.

"Yeah!" said the girls.

Franco, Miss Westminster, and the girls all hurried out of Franco's office and began heading for the ballroom.

When they arrived, they started arranging the room for an international conference.

Suddenly the doors to the ballroom opened. There stood Luger Colt with his crossbow and Sammy Smith with his machine gun.

"Come in, gentlemen," said Miss Westminster.

Luger and Sammy came in.

Miss Westminster showed them to the conference table. "Have a seat, gentlemen, please," she said. "We have something very important to discuss with you."

Luger Colt sat down.

Sammy Smith sat down.

Miss Westminster and Franco sat down and faced them.

The girls all gathered around.

"Gentlemen," Miss Westminster began, "we understand that both your organizations are desirous of acquiring the services of . . ." Miss Westminster looked at Franco. Franco took a big gulp.

". . . of *Mr. Spaghetti Man.*"

Sammy Smith stood up. "He's ours!" he shouted.

Luger Colt stood up. "He's ours!" he shouted.

"Over my dead body!" shouted Sammy Smith.

"My pleasure!" shouted Luger Colt.

They grabbed each other by the necks and started choking one another.

"Gentlemen!" shouted Miss Westminster.

Sammy and Luger stopped choking each other and looked up.

"We are here to discuss a solution to your mutual problem," said Miss Westminster. "Please sit down!"

Sammy and Luger sat down.

"We have decided," continued Miss Westminster, "that the only way to settle this problem is to have an international conference just like they do in Geneva, Switzerland."

"That's fine," said Luger, "just as long as we win!"

"The same goes for us!" said Sammy.

"You gentlemen could use one of my courses in International Conference Manners!" said Miss Westminster.

The girls groaned.

Sammy and Luger looked chastised.

"Now then," continued Miss Westminster, "that's better. I'd like to open this conference by having each of you gentlemen tell me when you first learned about this mysterious Mr. Spaghetti Man. We'll begin with Mr. Luger Colt, President of the Saintly Survivalist Sect. Mr. Colt."

Luger stood up. "We first heard of Mr. Spaghetti Man last week," he began. "One of our members was driving through Little Indian and he had to stop for gas. Well, this attendant told him a strange tale about a man hiding up in the mountains above Little Indian who knows the secret of how to make a whole lot of spaghetti!"

Miss Westminster and the girls glanced at Franco.

Franco had a puzzled look on his face.

"Do you know what this man looks like?" asked Miss Westminster.

"All we know is that he's a monster!" said Luger. "He has spaghetti growing all over him. He looks like a big pile of spaghetti with arms and legs and a head!"

Miss Westminster and the girls raised their eyebrows at Franco.

Franco had an even more puzzled look on his face.

"And did your member believe this service-station attendant's story?" asked Miss Westminster.

"Yes, ma'am," said Luger. "The attendant showed him a secret drawing he had made of Mr. Spaghetti Man."

"Thank you, Mr. Colt," said Miss Westminster.

Luger sat down.

"Now, Mr. Smith," said Miss Westminster, "we should like to hear your side of the story. Tell us when you first heard about this person you call Mr. Spaghetti Man and include in your statement—"

"I know, I know," said Sammy, interrupting, " 'and include in your statement blah . . . blah . . . blah . . .' "

"Well!" said Miss Westminster huffily.

Sammy stood up. "Well, you see," he began, "we first heard of Mr. Spaghetti Man a couple of weeks ago. We were passing through on our way to Albany and we stopped here in Little Indian at the service station, and this service-station attendant tells my buddy about this strange person covered with spaghetti who roams all around the mountains at night, you see. He showed us the same drawing too."

Miss Westminster and the girls were staring hard at Franco.

Franco's face showed even greater puzzlement.

Miss Westminster stood up. "Franco, please stand next to me," she said. Franco stood next to Miss Westminster. "I think you need professional help," she whispered. Then she looked at Luger and Sammy. "Gentlemen," she said, "before you stands . . ." She cleared her throat. ". . . Mr. Spaghetti Man, and I have now decided who . . ."

Luger looked at Franco.

Sammy looked at Franco.

They both started laughing hysterically. "Ha-ha-ha-ha-ha-ha-ha-ha-ha-ha-ha-ha-ha-ha-ha-ha-ha-ha-ha-ha!"

"He's not Mr. Spaghetti Man!" said Luger.

"He's not Mr. Spaghetti Man!" said Sammy.

Miss Westminster looked at Franco. "What do they mean?" she asked.

"There really may be another Mr. Spaghetti Man," said Franco.

Miss Westminster blinked. "What do *you* mean?" she said.

"I've heard all those stories too," explained Franco, "but I always thought they were just talking about me."

"And you didn't tell me?" said Miss Westminster. "You mean you let me go through all this for nothing?"

Franco shrugged.

"Well, . . . what about the *monster* part?" asked Miss Westminster.

"Yeah!" said the girls.

"Oh, you know how people are always making up stories about celebrities," said Franco

Whack! Whack! Whack!

"What was that?" asked Miss Westminster. She looked up. Three meatballs were stuck on the ceiling directly above her.

Splat! Splat! Splat!

Miss Westminster looked down. Franco, Sammy, and Luger were covered with spaghetti sauce.

Swish! Swish! Swish!

Miss Westminster whirled around. The girls were completely gagged and bound by long strands of spaghetti.

"What the . . ." Miss Westminster started to say, but then she saw the GAFIA and the SSS. They were standing at opposite ends of the ballroom with armloads of spaghetti, handfuls of meatballs, and big pots of spaghetti sauce.

Whack! Splat! Swish!

"*Aaaaagggggghhhhh!*" screamed Miss Westminster. "Look at this gook all over my conference dress! It's ruined."

Franco looked up. Spaghetti sauce was running down his face. "I'll have you know that that 'gook' is my secret spaghetti sauce!" he said.

"Well, excu-u-u-u-se me!" said Miss Westminster.

Luger jumped up and hurriedly wiped the spaghetti sauce off his face, his Brunton Rubber Armored 8 × 30 binoculars, and his Brunton Model 8040 compass. "It's war!" he screamed. Then he grabbed his crossbow and rushed toward the SSS end of the ballroom.

Sammy jumped up and hurriedly wiped the spaghetti sauce off his black leisure suit; then he picked up his machine gun and ran to the GAFIA end of the ballroom.

"Fire!" screamed Luger.

"Fire!" screamed Sammy.

The SSS and the GAFIA began throwing spaghetti and meatballs at each other and dumping spaghetti sauce onto the floor. *Whack! Splat! Swish! Slurp! Whack! Splat! Swish! Slurp!*

Franco, Miss Westminster, and the girls were caught in the middle.

"Hit the deck!" screamed Miss Westminster.

Franco and Miss Westminster fell to the floor, but the girls couldn't move because of the spaghetti wrapped around them.

The spaghetti and meatballs continued to fly through the air. The spaghetti sauce continued to flood the ballroom floor. *Whack! Splat! Swish! Slurp! Whack! Splat! Swish! Slurp!*

Franco and Miss Westminster stood up again and began unraveling the girls.

Whack! Splat! Swish! Slurp! Whack! Splat! Swish! Slurp!

Finally, the girls were freed of their spaghetti bonds. Everybody fell to the floor and began sliding through the spaghetti sauce that had now reached them.

"I can't stop sliding!" screamed Miss Westminster.

"Me either!" screamed Franco.

"Whee!" shouted the girls. "This is fun!"

"Charge!" screamed Luger.

"Charge!" screamed Sammy.

The GAFIA and the SSS began rushing toward each other.

The spaghetti and meatballs continued to fly through the air. The spaghetti sauce continued to rise higher and higher. *Whack! Splat! Swish! Slurp! Whack! Splat! Swish! Slurp!*

Luger speared several hundred meatballs with his crossbow. *Twang! Twang! Twang! Twang! Twang! Twang!*

Sammy machine-gunned several hundred meatballs to the wall. *Rat-a-tat! Splat! Splat! Rat-a-tat! Splat! Splat!*

The girls were now swimming laps through the spaghetti sauce.

"What are we going to do?" shouted Franco to Miss Westminster.

"I have an idea!" shouted Miss Westminster back. She began swimming toward the microphone. She reached it, grabbed it, and opened her mouth to speak. But she got a meatball instead. "Not half bad!" she said. When she was through eating the meatball, she grabbed for the microphone again. *"Truce!"* she shouted.

The GAFIA and the SSS stopped fighting and looked at Miss Westminster. *"Truce?"* they shouted back.

"That's right!" shouted Miss Westminster. "I am declaring a truce. You will fight no more . . . or at least not until further notice!" To Franco and the girls, she shouted, "Come on, let's get out of here!"

CHAPTER NINE

The Pasta Nostra
to the Rescue

"Do you think the truce will hold?" Franco asked Miss Westminster.

"Are you kidding?" said Miss Westminster. "The GAFIA and the SSS will be at each others' throats before we can turn around, if we don't do something else!"

"What did you have in mind?" asked Merridith.

"We need to have an International Italian Spaghetti Summit Meeting!" said Miss Westminster.

The girls groaned.

"If a *conference* failed," said Franco, "what makes you think a *summit* meeting would succeed?"

"Breeding!" said Miss Westminster.

"Yeah!" said the girls.

"Oh," said Franco. "Anything else?"

"Yes," said Miss Westminster, "and if we arrange the room properly, and if we invite the world press, and . . ."

". . . if we do something about the land mines and the machine-gun nests," added Fredonia.

"Good heavens!" said Miss Westminster. "I forgot about those! We could have all been blown to smithereens!"

"But what *else* can we do, Miss Westminster?" asked Augusta. "Now we don't even know who Mr. Spaghetti Man is!"

"Yeah!" said Carla and Marla.

"We need a totally unbiased opinion in this matter," said Miss Westminster. "We need somebody to mediate."

"Who did you have in mind?" asked Loretta.

"Whom!" said Miss Westminster.

"I don't know," said Loretta, "that's why I'm asking you."

Miss Westminster cleared her throat. "We need somebody who knows everything there is to know about spaghetti," she said. "That person would be able to tell us what to do."

"Well, I can try," said Franco, "but . . ."

"I wasn't thinking about you," said Miss Westminster.

"Oh," said Franco.

"I was thinking about the Pasta Nostra," said Miss Westminster.

Franco gasped. "You mean, *the* Pasta Nostra?"

"Aren't they the ones who ran Mama Rosa out of business?" said Loretta.

"Yeah!" said Fredonia.

"Who's Mama Rosa?" asked Franco.

"She's the lady we met in prison," said Merridith.

"What?" said Franco.

"Nothing!" said Miss Westminster.

"Well," said Franco, "it just sounds so . . . . . . frightening, that's all, getting involved with the Pasta Nostra."

"I know it does," said Miss Westminster, "but who else in the world knows more about spaghetti?"

"I suppose you're right," said Franco.

"Of course I'm right," said Miss Westminster. "If you're involved in international affairs, you have to take chances. I think I'll telephone Mr. Presidente at the Pasta Nostra World Headquarters in Venice, Italy, and invite him to come to Little Indian to solve this problem for us."

"Do you know him?" asked Franco.

"Well, I wrote him a letter once," said Miss Westminster. "We needed some pasta samples for our Italian class. He probably remembers me."

"Well, come on then," said Merridith. "We've got to get started right away before there's another spaghetti-and-meatball war!"

"Ah jus' don't think Ah could stand another spaghetti-and-meatball war," said Augusta.

"Us either," said Carla and Marla.

"I'll do it right away," said Miss Westminster. She walked over

57

to the telephone, looked up the access code for Italy, and dialed. After a few minutes, she said, "I'd like to speak to Mr. Presidente, please." Then she said, "Well, it's okay, you can wake him up. He won't mind. Just tell him it's Gertie Westminster calling from America." Miss Westminster looked at Franco and the girls and smiled. "Hello, Mr. Presidente. How are you? I'm sure you remember the letter I sent you a couple of years ago when we needed some pasta samples for our Italian class—well, this call has nothing to do with that. You see, we're all up here in Little Indian, New York, and we have a spaghetti-and-meatball war on our hands. You see . . . Yes, I said spaghetti-and-meatball war. Well, it seems that there is this mysterious Mr. Spaghetti Man who evidently knows a secret that will either destroy or revolutionize the spaghetti industry, and the GAFIA and the SSS are both trying to find him. We've got to do something before there's another war! It occurred to me that the Pasta Nostra might be able to settle this matter once and for all at an International Italian Spaghetti Summit Meeting. What do you say, Mr. Presidente? Okay . . . okay . . . okay . . . okay . . . unhuh . . . unhuh . . . unhuh . . . unhuh . . . well, that's just super, Mr. Presidente. And tell Mrs. Presidente that she can come along too. Okay . . . unhuh . . . okay . . . unhuh. Well, it sure has been nice talking to you, and we'll see you soon." She hung up the receiver and turned toward Franco and the girls.

"Well?" said Franco.

"Well?" said the girls.

"The Pasta Nostra is moving its World Headquarters to Little Indian for the summer," said Miss Westminster triumphantly. "They arrive tomorrow, and they'll be staying here at the inn! Mr. and Mrs. Presidente and 498 Pasta Nostra Executives!"

"Yea!" cried the girls.

Franco gasped. "What are we going to do?"

"We're going to do it *right* this time," said Miss Westminster. She turned to Fredonia. "Fredonia, I want you to be in charge of decorating the table. You will need to design flags for the GAFIA and the SSS. They always have these little flags in front of the delegates. It's so cute!"

"Okay," said Fredonia.

58

"And Loretta," continued Miss Westminster, "you'll need to have pitchers of water and several glasses handy."

"Okay," said Loretta.

"It can't just be plain, ordinary water either," said Merridith. "It has to be mineral water. My dad always has mineral water at the summits he attends in Europe."

Miss Westminster looked at Franco.

Franco swallowed hard. "No mineral water," he said. "It's too expensive!"

"Just plain water, Loretta," said Miss Westminster, "that's good enough!"

"We'll need ashtrays too," said Carla and Marla.

"Ah'll set out the ashtrays," said Augusta.

"No smoking at this summit meeting!" screamed Miss Westminster.

"Well, what *can* I do then?" whined Augusta.

"You *may* help Loretta serve the water," said Miss Westminster.

"Do you want us to fix a spaghetti-and-meatball dinner for everybody?" asked Carla and Marla.

"Are you kidding?" said Miss Westminster. "I don't want *any* food within a hundred miles of the ballroom during this summit meeting!"

"Yeah," said Franco, "I'll never get that ballroom cleaned up!"

"So there's nothing for us to do?" asked Carla and Marla.

"Nonsense! I want you two to be the Press Representatives," said Miss Westminster. "You are to notify all the press organizations in the world and then give them hourly briefings while we're at the summit meeting."

"Okay," said Carla and Marla.

"You'd better start reading some newspapers and magazines," added Miss Westminster, "so you'll know how to talk."

"Okay," said Carla and Marla.

"Merridith," said Miss Westminster, "I want you to translate the summit proceedings into any language that is necessary."

"Okay, Miss Westminster," said Merridith. "I know Russian and I'm learning Basque."

"Carla and Marla," said Miss Westminster, "maybe you'd better send a special invitation to Moscow about this summit meeting.

That way we can't be accused of taking sides. I'm not so sure about the Basques though. I think there are some living in California." She looked at Merridith. "Maybe you'd better go ahead and draft a news release in Basque anyway. It won't hurt to have one handy just in case."

"Check!" said Merridith.

Miss Westminster looked at Franco. "Your job is to dig up the land mines and take down the machine-gun nests," she said. "Here's a map showing the secret locations."

Franco paled. "I can't do that!" he said. "I'm a very nervous person!"

Miss Westminster shrugged. "Well," she said, "this summit meeting will be taking place on your property. If anybody gets blown to smithereens, you're the one who'll get sued!"

Franco sagged. Then he took the map from Miss Westminster. "Is this *before* or *after* I clean up the mess in the ballroom?" he asked.

"Before," said Miss Westminster.

Franco sighed deeply. "My last will and testament is in the bottom left-hand drawer of my desk," he said as he headed for the door.

"Okay, girls," said Miss Westminster brightly, "you all know your jobs! Let's get started!"

When they got to the ballroom, they had to step around thousands of meatballs and millions of spaghetti strands, but most of the spaghetti sauce had already drained off.

Loretta and Augusta set water pitchers and glasses around the summit table.

Fredonia designed and sewed up the GAFIA and SSS flags.

Merridith wrote news releases in Russian and Basque and gave them to Carla and Marla.

Carla and Marla telephoned UPI, AP, ABC, CBS, NBC, CNN, CBC, BBC, Reuters, and all the other press associations in Europe, Asia, Australia, Africa, North America, South America, and Antarctica.

Miss Westminster walked around the ballroom inspecting all the work.

Two hours later, Miss Westminster said, "Well, I think we're ready." She looked around the ballroom. "All that's left is for Franco to shovel out the spaghetti and meatballs and to mop up what's left of the spaghetti sauce."

The next morning, Augusta looked out the bedroom window and shouted, "We're being invaded!"

Miss Westminster and the girls rushed over to see what was happening. The skies above Little Indian were covered with red-, white-, and green-striped parachutes.

"They'll never take me alive!" screamed Merridith.

"Those are the colors of the Italian flag," said Fredonia.

"I bet it's the Pasta Nostra," said Loretta.

"But why didn't they just arrive in the normal way," asked Augusta, "on a connecting flight from Atlanta?"

Miss Westminster smiled. "Because the Pasta Nostra isn't normal," she said. "They do things differently!"

Miss Westminster and the girls hurriedly dressed and then rushed to the lobby. Franco was already there, looking out through the glass front doors.

Suddenly, 500 men and women burst through the door, dragging their parachutes behind them.

"Mr. and Mrs. Pasta Nostra Presidente?" asked Miss Westminster of the man and woman at the front of the group.

"Si," said Mr. and Mrs. Presidente.

"Welcome to Little Indian and to Franco's Famous Italian Spaghetti Inn and Overnight Campground!" said the girls.

"Grazie!" said Mr. and Mrs. Presidente.

"Is there a problem?" asked Franco, pointing to the parachutes. "Did you have plane trouble?"

"We couldn't land at Little Indian International Airport," said Mr. Presidente, "so we all had to parachute out instead!"

"Yes," said Mrs. Presidente, "somebody in Albany named Mad Mary wouldn't give us permission to land. She thought we were terrorists!"

"I might have known," muttered Franco. "Even when she's gone, she knows what's going on!"

"Well, you're all here now," said Miss Westminster, "so let's

61

not fret over little things. As soon as the reporters arrive, we can begin the summit meeting!''

"While we're waiting," said Mr. Presidente, "we can be digging the canals!''

Miss Westminster looked at Mr. Presidente and said, *"Canals?"*

"Of course," said Mr. Presidente. "How do you expect us to get around while we're here in Little Indian?''

"Couldn't you just use cars?" said Loretta.

"Silly *signorina!*" said Mrs. Presidente. "What would we do with all the gondolas we brought over here?''

"Gondolas?" said Fredonia.

"Yes," said Mr. Presidente. "Thank heavens we had parachutes for those too!''

"We just won't feel at home if we can't travel by gondola," said Mrs. Presidente. "After all, we *are* from Venice!''

Miss Westminster sighed. "Well, let's get started then!" she said.

"Wait a minute!" said Franco. "Don't you think we ought to check with Mad Mary first?''

"She's still in Albany, remember?" said Fredonia.

"Oh, yeah," said Franco. He thought for a minute. "Well, maybe she won't be too mad. At least there won't be any more traffic jams in Little Indian.''

"Well, what about all the people driving along Route Twenty-eight?" said Merridith. "How will they get through Little Indian?''

"Yeah," said Carla and Marla. "What about them?''

"Simple," said Mr. Presidente. "When they get to Little Indian, we'll just put them on a gondola ferry and take them to the end of the canal.''

"Ah've jus' never built a canal before," said Augusta. "Not even in Georgia!''

"Me either," said Loretta.

"Come on then," said Mr. Presidente, "I'll show you how." He began handing shovels to Franco, Miss Westminster, the girls, and the 498 Pasta Nostra Executives.

CHAPTER TEN

Renaissance in Little Indian

"What are we supposed to do with these?" asked Miss Westminster.

"Dig! Dig! Dig!" cried Mr. Presidente.

"On second thought, I really should be working on the International Italian Spaghetti Summit Meeting," said Miss Westminster. "There are always last-minute details to take care of!"

"Yeah!" said Franco and the girls.

"There won't be any International Italian Spaghetti Summit Meeting," said Mr. Presidente, "if there are no canals to get to it!"

So Franco, Miss Westminster, the girls, and the 498 Pasta Nostra Executives started digging.

Mr. and Mrs. Presidente began singing "O Solo Mio."

By midmorning, they had dug up half the street in front of the inn.

"Now, fill it full of water," said Mr. Presidente, "and we'll put in the first gondola!"

Franco attached the garden hose to the faucet in front of the inn and started filling up the canal.

"It's all muddy and yucky," said Loretta.

"Yes, yes," said Mrs. Presidente.

"We must put the first gondola into the canal," said Mr. Presidente. "Everybody take hold and lift it gently into the water!"

Everybody grabbed hold of the gondola and lifted it gently into the canal.

"There!" said Mr. Presidente. He had tears in his eyes.

Everybody cheered.

Mr. Presidente helped Mrs. Presidente aboard and then went aboard himself.

"Bring on the gondolier!" shouted Mrs. Presidente.

"We don't have a gondolier!" said Miss Westminster.

"We have to have a gondolier!" cried Mrs. Presidente.

"I can sing," said Loretta.

"But you're not dressed properly," said Mrs. Presidente. "Here, I just happen to have the proper outfit in my purse." She pulled out a gondolier's costume and handed it to Loretta. "Go inside the inn and change," she ordered.

"Yes, ma'am," said Loretta.

"What about us?" cried the other girls. "We can sing too!"

"But who will help the Pasta Nostra Executives dig the other canals?" asked Mr. Presidente.

Miss Westminster and the other girls sighed. Then they picked up their shovels again and started digging.

Loretta came out of the inn dressed as a gondolier. She got into the gondola and started paddling Mr. and Mrs. Presidente up and down the canal. She joined in singing "O Solo Mio" while she paddled.

As Miss Westminster, the girls, and the Pasta Nostra Executives finished a portion of the canal, Franco would fill it with water from the garden hose.

Finally, by noon, they had dug up the entire street in front of the inn and had filled it full of water.

Loretta had paddled back and forth across the canal several thousands of times.

Mr. and Mrs. Presidente were hoarse from singing "O Solo Mio."

Miss Westminster set down her shovel. "It'll take us years to dig up all the streets of Little Indian," she said.

"Yeah!" shouted the girls. They gave Loretta a dirty look.

"Well," said Mr. Presidente, "I suppose the Pasta Nostra Executives can dig the rest of the canals."

"Thank goodness," said Miss Westminster. "Come on, girls!"

"Wait a minute!" said Mr. Presidente. "We haven't painted the ceilings yet!"

"What ceilings?" asked Fredonia.

"All Italian buildings have pictures painted on the ceilings," said Mr. Presidente.

"Yes," said Mrs. Presidente. "We won't feel at home if we have to walk around in buildings that don't have paintings on the ceilings!"

"Yes," said Mr. Presidente, "we have to have sky and clouds and cherubs and seraphs and harps and things like that above us all the time!"

"Well, come on then," said Miss Westminster, "let's get started!"

"Why can't the GAFIA and the SSS help us paint the ceilings?" demanded Merridith.

"Yeah!" cried the other girls.

"They're on R and R," said Franco.

"What's R and R?" asked Carla and Marla.

"Rest and Relaxation," said Franco. "It's what you do after you've been in a spaghetti-and-meatball war."

"Well, Ah was in a spaghetti-and-meatball war too," said Augusta. "Ah need some R and R badly."

"Do you want me to sing while everyone else is painting?" asked Loretta.

"Grab a paintbrush!" everybody shouted.

"Where will we start?" asked Miss Westminster.

"We'll divide up the town," said Mr. Presidente as he and Mrs. Presidente and Loretta stepped off the gondola.

Miss Westminster looked at Franco. "Do you have a city map of Little Indian?"

"Here," said Franco, taking a map from his coat pocket. "Let's start on Main Street—I mean Main *Canal*—first. I suggest, Mr. Presidente, that Miss Westminster and the girls begin first with Big Bob's Friendly Used Car Showroom. It's a Little Indian landmark."

"Okay," said Mr. Presidente.

"Okay," said Miss Westminster and the girls.

"When you get through at Big Bob's," added Franco, "come back and we'll give you another place to paint."

Miss Westminster looked up the canal toward Big Bob's. "How will we get there?" she asked.

65

"Use the gondola," said Mr. Presidente. "That's why we have it!"

"Frankly, I think it would have been simpler to have used the sidewalk that used to be there," said Merridith.

Mr. and Mrs. Presidente gave her a dirty look.

"Do you have any pictures of what this ceiling is supposed to look like?" asked Miss Westminster.

"Yes," said Mr. Presidente, "it's supposed to look like these frescoes in the Ducal Palace in Venice!" He took a picture out of his wallet and handed it to Miss Westminster.

"Good heavens!" said Miss Westminster.

The girls all gathered around to look.

"You mean," said Merridith, "that we're supposed to paint pictures of naked ladies on the ceiling of Big Bob's Friendly Used Car Showroom?"

"Big Bob's not going to like that," said Franco.

"That's art!" cried Mr. Presidente.

"Yeah!" added Mrs. Presidente.

"Well, all right," said Miss Westminster. She and the girls picked up their paintbrushes and cans of paint and stepped aboard the gondola. Loretta paddled them to the end of the canal.

"Big Bob's is just up the street," said Miss Westminster. "We can use the sidewalk until this part of the canal is finished."

Big Bob looked up as Miss Westminster and the girls came into the building.

"Say, little ladies," said Big Bob, "what can I do for you today? You know, I've got this fire-engine red 1975 Chevrolet with mud flaps that's only had ten owners. You'd love it!"

"Actually, we're here to paint your ceiling," said Miss Westminster.

"Say, well, I don't remember hiring anybody to do that," said Big Bob.

"Oh, you didn't hire us," said Loretta. "Mr. Presidente of the Pasta Nostra sent us."

"He did? Well, that's different," said Big Bob. "Uh, how much is this going to set me back?"

"Oh, I don't suppose anything," said Miss Westminster.

"The Pasta Nostra is paying for it," said Fredonia.

66

Big Bob looked up at the ceiling. "Well, in that case," he said, "here's a ladder! Paint away!"

"Put the ladder over here, Loretta," said Miss Westminster.

"We want to paint the clouds," said Carla and Marla.

"I want to paint the cherubs," said Loretta.

"I want to paint the seraphs," said Augusta.

"I want to paint the harps," said Merridith.

"I want to paint the naked ladies," said Fredonia.

"Naked ladies?" said Big Bob. "What's going on here? I don't want any naked ladies on my ceiling. I want *blue!*"

"This is art," said Miss Westminster huffily.

"Say, well, I guess this place could use a little art," said Big Bob. "Maybe it'll attract business."

Miss Westminster moved the ladder to the center of the showroom. "We'll have to set up some scaffolding," she said. "Do you have another ladder?"

Big Bob got another ladder out of the back room and some boards and set up scaffolding that reached from one end of the showroom to the other.

Miss Westminster and the girls carried the paintbrushes and the paint to the top of the scaffolding, lay down on their backs, and began painting.

First they all painted the whole ceiling blue to represent the sky.

Next Carla and Marla painted the clouds.

"Those don't look like any clouds I've ever seen," complained Merridith.

"We know clouds," said Carla and Marla. "At home we lie around all the time looking at clouds."

"They look fine to me, girls," said Miss Westminster, "although do you think you could fleece up the ones on the west side?"

Carla and Marla looked. "Those are storm clouds," they said.

"Hmm," said Miss Westminster. "I don't remember ever seeing storm clouds on a fresco."

"This is a first," said Carla and Marla.

"Well, all right," said Miss Westminster. "Now, Augusta, you paint the seraphs."

"She'd better not mess up our clouds," said Carla and Marla.

"Ah don't mess up," said Augusta, "even in Georgia!"

"And Loretta, you paint the cherubs," continued Miss Westminster, "and Merridith, you paint the harps. I think this is going to look cute, don't you?"

"Say," said Big Bob, craning his neck to see, "this really does look kind of pretty."

"Thank you," said Miss Westminster.

"Thank you," said the girls.

"Now, Fredonia," said Miss Westminster, "since the next part of this fresco must be done with extremely good taste, I'll help you paint the young ladies *sans* clothing."

"You mean the *naked* ladies?" said Fredonia.

Miss Westminster cleared her throat. "I think we'll put them mostly behind the clouds," she said.

"Don't mess up our clouds," said Carla and Marla.

"How will anybody know they're naked if we put them behind the clouds?" asked Fredonia.

"Just do as I say, Fredonia!" said Miss Westminster.

Finally, the fresco was ready.

Big Bob peered up at the cherubs, the seraphs, the harps, and the two feet, two hands, and head of a lady sticking out from behind each of the clouds. "Say," he said, "I never knew that art could be so great! I've been missing a lot, hanging around all these used cars all my life. I think I could use some more of this!"

Miss Westminster beamed. Then she looked at the girls. "You're all covered with paint," she said.

"So are you," said Fredonia.

"You can clean up in the back washroom," said Big Bob.

"Thanks," said Miss Westminster.

She and the girls headed for the washroom.

"I'll get my salesmen to take down the scaffolding," said Big Bob. "It's the least I can do for you after all you've done for art!"

Inside the washroom, Fredonia said, "You know, I'm proud. Little Indian is having its own Renaissance, and we're a part of it!"

"I never thought of that," said Miss Westminster, as she washed the blue paint off her face. "It's just as though we were in Italy in the fourteenth century, at the rebirth of art and literature."

"We're making history today," said Augusta.

"I wonder if I'll be known as the Leonardo da Vinci of Little Indian," said Loretta.

"Why *you?*" said Merridith. "Did you see those harps I painted? I'd put my harps up against anybody's harps!"

"Girls, girls," said Miss Westminster, "you can all be proud of what you've accomplished today!"

When they had all cleaned up, Miss Westminster and the girls went back into the showroom to say good-bye to Big Bob. A crowd of people had formed and Big Bob was in the center of it, explaining art. He motioned to Miss Westminster to come over.

"I was right," said Big Bob.

"About what?" asked Miss Westminster.

"Just look at this!" said Big Bob. He pointed to the crowd. "I bet they're all here to buy used cars. Isn't it wonderful?"

"Wonderful!" said Miss Westminster. "But where do they plan to drive them?"

"Yeah," said Loretta. "Don't they know that Little Indian doesn't have streets anymore?"

Big Bob had a stricken look on his face, but before he could say anything, he was pulled back into the crowd and disappeared from sight.

"Come on, girls," said Miss Westminster, "we've got to get out of here before we're crushed."

Miss Westminster and the girls hurried back down Main Street until they reached Main Canal. A gondola with a new gondolier was waiting for them.

"I guess I've been replaced," muttered Loretta as they all got aboard.

"I wonder what else the Pasta Nostra has planned for us," said Merridith.

"There's no telling," said Miss Westminster.

The gondola hit the opposite bank with a bang and Miss Westminster and the girls almost fell into the canal.

Mr. and Mrs. Presidente were waiting for them on shore.

"Well, how did the painting go?" asked Mr. Presidente.

"Fine," said Miss Westminster. "Big Bob was very happy with the results."

"He had a big crowd there when we left," said Fredonia.

"Well, that makes me very happy," said Mr. Presidente.

Miss Westminster looked at Mr. Presidente. "Uh, was there anything else you wanted us to do?" she asked.

Mr. Presidente looked at Mrs. Presidente. "Dear?" he said.

"Well I *am* beginning to feel at home," said Mrs. Presidente.

Miss Westminster and the girls looked expectantly again at Mr. Presidente.

Mr. Presidente said, "Well, I guess we're at a point where the Pasta Nostra Executives can finish digging the rest of the canals and painting the rest of the ceilings."

"Yea!" cried Miss Westminster and the girls.

Mr. Presidente smiled and said, "The International Italian Spaghetti Summit Meeting may begin in the morning!"

"But the reporters aren't here yet!" cried Carla and Marla.

"I guess the world press isn't interested in our summit meeting," said Fredonia.

"Yeah," said the other girls.

"Don't worry," said Miss Westminster, "I'll have this all taken care of before morning!"

CHAPTER ELEVEN

The International Italian Spaghetti Summit Meeting

"Wake up!" screamed Augusta.

Miss Westminster and the other girls opened their eyes.

"What's wrong?" asked Miss Westminster.

"We're being invaded again," said Augusta. "Look out the window!"

Parachutes again covered the skies over Little Indian.

"What's going on *now?*" asked Fredonia.

"I think I know," said Miss Westminster. "Come on, girls, we must hurry up and get dressed!"

"Yeah, we may have to escape," said Merridith, "because *they'll never take me alive!"*

Miss Westminster and the girls got dressed and then rushed downstairs. Franco was already in the lobby. Just then, several hundred people burst through the front door. They were dragging parachutes behind them.

"Who are you people?" asked Franco.

"I'm Jacques Jacques," said the first man through. He started taking off his parachute and jumpsuit. "I represent the French Press. Are we too late to cover the end of the world?"

"What?" exclaimed Franco.

"What?" exclaimed the girls.

Miss Westminster turned red.

"What are you talking about?" said Fredonia.

"We each received an anonymous telephone call last night that the end of the world would take place here in Little Indian this morning," explained Jacques Jacques. "Are we too late?"

Franco and the girls looked at Miss Westminster.

Miss Westminster turned even redder. "Well, it's not exactly the end of the world yet," she said, "but it *is* the International Italian Spaghetti Summit Meeting, and if it's not held soon, it may really be the end of the world as we know it!"

"Well, I'm sure we're all somewhat disappointed," said Jacques Jacques, "but since we're already here, we might as well cover the summit meeting."

Miss Westminster let out a sigh of relief. Then she turned to the girls. "Quick, go tell the GAFIA, the SSS, and the Pasta Nostra to get dressed and come to the ballroom," she said. "The International Italian Spaghetti Summit Meeting is about to begin!"

The girls rushed off in different directions.

The lobby continued to fill up with men and women in jumpsuits, with parachutes dragging behind them. Soon 1,000 people jammed the lobby.

"Why did you people parachute into Little Indian?" shouted Franco. "Why didn't you just arrive in the normal way?"

"Somebody in Albany named Mad Mary wouldn't give us permission to land," said a reporter from Portugal. "She thought we were terrorists!"

"Oh no, not again," said Franco. "That woman will absolutely destroy tourism in Little Indian!"

"Okay, Miss Westminster," shouted Fredonia, "we're all ready!"

Franco and Miss Westminster led the 1,000 reporters into the ballroom. The GAFIA, the SSS, and the Pasta Nostra were already seated.

"Carla, Marla, get busy!" shouted Miss Westminster. "Take care of the reporters!"

"Okay, Miss Westminster!" shouted Carla and Marla. They checked the reporters' credentials, gave them a short briefing, then seated them all on the floor.

Miss Westminster and Franco joined Sammy, Luger, and Mr. Presidente at the summit table.

Then Miss Westminster nodded to Fredonia.

Fredonia came to the microphone. "Will everybody please stand so we may say the Pledge of Allegiance to the flags of the GAFIA and the SSS?"

Everybody stood.

But nobody said a word.

"What's wrong?" whispered Miss Westminster.

"We don't have a Pledge of Allegiance," said Luger.

"We don't either," said Sammy.

Miss Westminster said, "Thank you very much. You may all be seated."

Everybody sat down.

Miss Westminster looked out over the audience again. "We have decided to have this high-level summit meeting, just as they do in Geneva, Switzerland," she began, "in order to settle a matter which could have led to the end of the world!"

"Yeah!" said Sammy.

"Yeah!" said Luger.

The reporters took notes furiously.

"Does anybody know the word for 'yeah' in Basque?" asked Merridith.

"As chairperson of this International Italian Spaghetti Summit Meeting," began Miss Westminster, "I . . ."

Merridith grabbed the microphone and began translating into Basque.

When she had finished, Miss Westminster asked, "Are you sure that there are some Basques here?"

"Yeah, there's a reporter here from a little town in California who has his Basque grandfather with him," said Merridith. "I want to make sure he understands everything."

"Well, all right," said Miss Westminster, "but why don't you just sort of summarize from time to time?"

"I'm just trying to do my job, Miss Westminster," said Merridith with a pout.

Miss Westminster turned back to the audience. "As I was saying," she continued, "we have called this International Italian Spaghetti Summit Meeting to solve the problem of who gets to talk to Mr. Spaghetti Man first . . ."

The GAFIA stood up and shouted, "We do!"

The SSS stood up and shouted, "We do!"

The reporters took notes furiously.

Merridith hurriedly translated into Basque.

"Sit down!" shouted Miss Westminster.

Everybody sat down.

"I'll have no more of these outbursts!" said Miss Westminster. She took a deep breath. "We are here to solve the problem of who gets to talk to Mr. Spaghetti Man first about his secret."

The GAFIA and the SSS started to stand up again, but Miss Westminster shook her fist at them. They remained seated.

"We have invited Mr. Presidente of the Pasta Nostra here to settle this matter," continued Miss Westminster, "because we asked ourselves, Who knows more about spaghetti than the Pasta Nostra?"

"Yea! Yea!" cheered the Pasta Nostra.

"I should now like to turn these proceedings over to Mr. Presidente so he can solve this problem," said Miss Westminster.

"Yea! Yea!" cheered the Pasta Nostra.

The reporters took notes furiously.

Merridith hurriedly translated into Basque.

Mr. Presidente came to the microphone. "We in the Pasta Nostra are honored to have been asked to solve this problem and at the same time to bring some badly needed culture to Little Indian," he began. "Look around you and you will see our influence everywhere! You can now travel by canal all over Little Indian. You can now look up at the ceilings of every building in Little Indian and see frescoes. Little Indian is now Little Italy!"

"Yea! Yea!" cheered the Pasta Nostra.

"But the real reason we are here," continued Mr. Presidente, "is to settle the dispute between the GAFIA and the SSS over who gets to talk to Mr. Spaghetti Man first about his secret. I'll now invite Sammy Smith, President of the GAFIA, to come tell us his side of this story. Sammy, will you please come forward?"

The GAFIA stood up and cheered.

The SSS stood up and booed.

The reporters took notes furiously.

Merridith hurriedly translated into Basque.

Sammy Smith took hold of the microphone. "We appreciate you

74

Pasta Nostra people coming over here," he began. "We want you to know that. You see, it's very important that we talk to this–here Mr. Spaghetti Man first. We think he can help us make the best spaghetti in the world. Then we're going to sell it. at the lowest possible price and put all the other spaghetti people out of business. Then we're going to raise our prices and get rich. Anybody who wants spaghetti will have to come to us, because we'll control the spaghetti industry. The GAFIA will then be the most important organization in the world!"

The GAFIA stood up and cheered.

"So, Mr. Presidente," continued Sammy Smith, "we in the GAFIA hope that you will rule in favor of us!"

The GAFIA stood up again and cheered.

The SSS stood up and booed.

The reporters took notes furiously.

"That was an incredible presentation," said Augusta. "Ah don't remember when Ah have ever been so moved!"

"I agree," said Merridith. Then she hurriedly translated everything into Basque.

Mr. Presidente came to the microphone again. "Thank you, Mr. Sammy Smith, President of the GAFIA, for your presentation," he said. "Now we'll hear from Mr. Luger Colt, President of the Saintly Survivalist Sect."

The SSS stood up and cheered.

The GAFIA stood up and booed.

The reporters took notes furiously.

Merridith hurriedly translated into Basque.

Luger Colt strutted up to the microphone. "Hey, I mean, you know," he began, "we appreciate the GAFIA's position and all that, but we need this-here Mr. Spaghetti Man too, because we have to survive, you know. You see, this-here invasion's coming, and we have to be ready, you see, because we're going to stockpile all the spaghetti we can, so we need this Mr. Spaghetti Man's secret so we can feed all of our people, you know, when this-here invasion comes, and then we'll have food and you won't, because if you're not for us, you're against us!"

The SSS stood up and cheered.

The GAFIA stood up and booed.

The reporters took notes furiously.

Merridith hurriedly translated into Basque.

"So, say," continued Luger, "that's about all I have on my mind, Mr. Presidente, so I hope you'll rule in favor of the SSS, you know what I mean, because if you're not for us, you're against us!"

The SSS stood up again and cheered.

"Bravo!" shouted Carla and Marla. "What a super job!"

The GAFIA stood up again and booed.

Luger Colt strutted back to his seat.

The reporters took notes furiously.

Merridith hurriedly translated into Basque.

Mr. Presidente took the microphone again. "I have listened carefully to both sides of this issue," he said, "and I have now decided that the first group to get to talk to Mr. Spaghetti Man about his incredible secret should be the . . . the . . . *Pasta Nostra!*"

The Pasta Nostra stood up and cheered.

The GAFIA remained silent.

The SSS remained silent.

The reporters remained silent.

Franco and Miss Westminster remained silent.

But Fredonia stood up and shouted, "I agree with the decision! I'm for the Pasta Nostra!"

"Me too!" shouted Loretta.

"Not us!" shouted Carla and Marla. "We think the SSS should get to talk to Mr. Spaghetti Man first!"

"Not me!" shouted Merridith. "I think it should go to the GAFIA!"

"Me too!" shouted Augusta. "They gave the best presentation!"

"Girls, girls, girls!" cried Miss Westminster. "What's come over you?"

But the girls didn't hear her. They had rushed onto the ballroom floor to take sides!

Miss Westminster said, "My whole world is falling apart!"

CHAPTER TWELVE

Mr. Spaghetti Man Comes Forward

Franco knocked on the door of Miss Westminster's room.

"Come in," said Miss Westminster.

Franco opened the door. Miss Westminster was lying on the bed watching the television news.

"I just wanted to tell you how sorry I am that all of your pupils defected," said Franco.

"Yes," said Miss Westminster, "all that expensive training down the drain!"

"Yeah," said Franco. He sighed. "Well, what do you plan to do now?"

"I don't know," said Miss Westminster, "but . . . wait a minute!" She sat up. "That's it!"

"What's it?" said Franco.

"I'm going to go on television," said Miss Westminster, "right here in Little Indian, and ask Mr. Spaghetti Man to come forward!"

"Say," said Franco, "that's a great idea, but will he do it?"

"I don't know," said Miss Westminster, "but maybe I can appeal to his patriotism or something."

"What do you plan to say?" asked Franco.

"I'm not quite sure," said Miss Westminster, "but we have to do something. Look at the problem we have. We have lost six fine young ladies for whose lives I was responsible. We have the GAFIA, the SSS, and now the Pasta Nostra almost at war and it's all because of an argument over who will get to talk to Mr. Spaghetti Man about his secret. Who else can solve this problem but Mr. Spaghetti Man himself?"

"Brilliant!" said Franco.

"Take me to the television station!" said Miss Westminster.

"That'll be WYUK, Little Indian's award-winning television station," said Franco.

Franco and Miss Westminster rushed downstairs and boarded a gondola in front of the inn.

"Take us to the studios of WYUK," said Franco to the gondolier.

After ten verses of "O Solo Mio," they arrived.

"We'll go see my friend, Smilin' Jack Jackson, Little Indian's award-winning newscaster," said Franco. "He'll be able to help us."

Smilin' Jack was between commercials when Franco and Miss Westminster walked into the studio. Franco introduced Miss Westminster and hurriedly told Smilin' Jack what the problem was.

Smilin' Jack yelled to his producer, "Hold the typhoon, hold the hurricane, hold the earthquake, hold the war! We've got the story of the century right here!"

The makeup lady hurriedly put makeup on Miss Westminster, and Smilin' Jack escorted her in front of the camera just as the commercial ended.

Smilin' Jack looked straight into the camera and said, "We've canceled the rest of the news, ladies and gentlemen, because we have a lady here in the studio whose story will break your hearts." He turned to Miss Westminster and with tears in his eyes said, "It's all yours, Gert!"

Miss Westminster said, "Thanks, Smilin' Jack." Then she turned toward the camera. "I am calling on Mr. Spaghetti Man to come forward," she began and then choked up. Smilin' Jack put his hand on her shoulder. "We know that you're out there somewhere within the range of my voice," continued Miss Westminster, "but only you know who you are and where you are. It is very important that you come forward, Mr. Spaghetti Man! We don't care how ugly you look. We don't care if you are covered with spaghetti. The lives of six innocent young girls hang in the balance, and only you have the power to save them and to prevent another spaghetti-and-meat-

78

ball war among the GAFIA, the SSS, and the Pasta Nostra. Only you can decide to whom you want to give your incredible spaghetti secret. I beg you, Mr. Spaghetti Man, to come forward at once from your secret hideout in the mountains above Little Indian and heal the nation's wounds! If you can hear me, then follow your heart by calling . . .'' Miss Westminster looked at Smilin' Jack.

Through tears, Smilin' Jack said, "555-3249."

". . . 555-3249," continued Miss Westminster. She smiled into the camera. "Thank you," she said.

"We're off the air!" shouted the producer.

Crying could be heard throughout the studio.

A telephone rang.

The producer answered it. "It's him," he shouted. "It's Mr. Spaghetti Man! He wants to talk to Miss Westminster!"

CHAPTER THIRTEEN

Trapped!

Miss Westminster grabbed the telephone from the producer's hands. "Hello! Hello!" she said breathlessly.

"Hello," said a man's voice slowly.

"Are you Mr. Spaghetti Man?" asked Miss Westminster.

"I think so," said the voice.

"What do you mean, you *think* so?" said Miss Westminster.

"Well, I was watching television," said the man, "and I saw you, and I started listening, and all of a sudden things started coming back to me, you know: that I had probably become a mad scientist whose life was dominated by an incredible spaghetti secret, and I do live in a secret hideout next to a little babbling brook in the mountains above Little Indian . . ."

"*Yippee, it's Mr. Spaghetti Man!*" screamed Miss Westminster. Then she cleared her throat and became more dignified.

"But . . ." said Mr. Spaghetti Man.

"But *what?*" demanded Miss Westminster.

"One thing bothers me," said Mr. Spaghetti Man.

"What's that?" asked Miss Westminster.

"Well, I'm not covered with spaghetti the way you said I would be," said Mr. Spaghetti Man.

"Well, that must just be a legend," said Miss Westminster. "Everything else fits!"

"Then I guess I'm the person you're appealing to," said Mr. Spaghetti Man. "I'm sorry I'm causing so much trouble. I'm not sure how I got up here in the mountains—that part's still pretty fuzzy—but I guess I should do what I can to heal the nation's wounds."

80

Miss Westminster flushed. "Well, it's not exactly the *nation's* wounds," she said. "I may have exaggerated that just a tad."

"Oh, really?" said Mr. Spaghetti Man. "Well, what is it that needs healing then?"

"Well, it's my girls," said Miss Westminster. "They've defected! You see, I'm the Headmistress of Miss Westminster's Fine School for Girls of Elizabeth, New Jersey, and we came up here to Little Indian to try out for Broadway, but then the GAFIA, the SSS, and the Pasta Nostra showed up and they *all* want you!"

"It sounds kind of complicated," said Mr. Spaghetti Man.

"Oh, it is," said Miss Westminster, "it really is! You know, Mr. Spaghetti Man, if you could just come forward and meet me somewhere, I could explain all this to you in person, and I wouldn't have to do it over the telephone. What do you say?"

"Well, I usually come down to Little Indian only late at night," said Mr. Spaghetti Man. "Would that be all right?"

"Yes, yes, that would be fine," said Miss Westminster. "How about meeting me late *tonight?*"

"All right," said Mr. Spaghetti Man, "but it'll have to be in a secluded place. I can't stand crowds!"

"What about the Little Indian Secluded Italian Restaurant?" said Miss Westminster. "Do you know it?"

"Yes, I know it," said Mr. Spaghetti Man. "I'll take the bus."

"Uh, well, I'm afraid the busses don't run anymore in Little Indian," said Miss Westminster. "You'll have to take a gondola."

"My, my, things have really changed in Little Indian since I was there last week," said Mr. Spaghetti Man.

"You have no idea!" said Miss Westminster.

"You know, everything is slowly coming back to me," said Mr. Spaghetti Man. "This secret of mine will change the world as we know it!"

Miss Westminster could hardly contain her excitement. "Good," she said. "I'll meet you at ten P.M. tonight at the Little Indian Secluded Italian Restaurant, all right?"

"All right," said Mr. Spaghetti Man. "I'll be there."

Miss Westminster heard a click as Mr. Spaghetti Man hung up the receiver.

Then she heard a second click.

81

She turned. "Is this line tapped?" she said.

"Yes, but don't worry about it," said Smilin' Jack. "Mad Mary has tapped all the phone lines in Little Indian."

"Well, all right," said Miss Westminster. She looked at Franco. "We must hurry back to the inn so I can get ready for a monumental secret meeting! This could be a turning point in the history of Western Civilization!"

"Be careful, Gert," said Smilin' Jack.

"I shall," said Miss Westminster.

Miss Westminster and Franco left the television station and boarded a gondola outside.

When they docked in front of the inn, Franco said, "Do you want me to go with you?"

"No, no," said Miss Westminster, "Mr. Spaghetti Man doesn't like crowds."

"Well, all right," said Franco, "whatever you say."

The inn seemed strangely quiet.

Miss Westminster bounded up the stairs, took a quick shower, then jumped into her crimson crepe dress. She grabbed her matching umbrella and began putting on her pumps as she bounded back down the center staircase.

The inn seemed even quieter.

Franco was nowhere in sight.

A gondola was docked in front. Miss Westminster hopped aboard. "Take me to the Little Indian Secluded Italian Restaurant!" she said to the short, fat gondolier.

"Si, signora," said the gondolier. He adjusted his bushy moustache and began singing "O Solo Mio."

"You look familiar," said Miss Westminster.

"Really?" said the gondolier.

The gondola finally docked in front of the restaurant and Miss Westminster hopped off.

"Arrivederci!" said the gondolier.

"Arrivederci!" said Miss Westminster. She walked up to the front of the restaurant and looked at the menu. Then she opened the door and went inside. "O Solo Mio" was playing softly. It was dark, but in the center of the dining room, Miss Westminster could see several very large plants. All the tables around them were empty.

"Si, signora?" said a voice.

Miss Westminster turned, startled. A short, fat waiter with a bushy moustache was standing behind her.

"Uh . . . I'm expecting somebody," said Miss Westminster, "but I don't see him . . . uh . . . this person."

"There is a very strange man seated at one of the tables in the center of the dining room," said the waiter.

Miss Westminster peered into the darkened interior again. "Where?" she asked. "I still don't see him."

"That's because he's sitting at the table in the middle of all those big plants," said the waiter.

"Uh, well, then, that's probably the person I'm here to see," said Miss Westminster. "Will you please take me to him?"

"Certainly, *signora,*" said the waiter. He adjusted his bushy moustache. "This way, please."

Miss Westminster began following him. "You look familiar," she said.

"Really?" said the waiter.

When they reached the center of the dining room, the waiter parted the big plants and Miss Westminster stepped through.

Seated alone at a table in the center was a thin young man. He looked nervous. But he didn't look strange. And he wasn't covered with spaghetti either. But there *was* something about his eyes.

The man looked up. Then he stood up. "Are you Miss Westminster?" he said.

"Yes," said Miss Westminster. "Are you Mr. Spaghetti Man?"

"Yes," said Mr. Spaghetti Man. He smiled.

Miss Westminster smiled. "It's a pleasure to meet you at long last," she said.

"Same here," said Mr. Spaghetti Man.

The waiter pulled out Miss Westminster's chair and she sat down at the table. "Would you care to order now?" he asked.

Miss Westminster looked at Mr. Spaghetti Man. "Would the Blue-Plate Special be all right with you?" she asked.

"Sure," said Mr. Spaghetti Man.

"Two," said Miss Westminster to the waiter.

"Two," said the waiter. Then he parted the big plants and left.

Miss Westminster looked into the strange eyes of Mr. Spaghetti Man and said, "So, what's new?"

"I don't get it," said Mr. Spaghetti Man.

"Uh, well, uh, what I mean is, how did you become Mr. Spaghetti Man?" stammered Miss Westminster.

"Well, I'm still not quite sure," said Mr. Spaghetti Man. "It's still kind of fuzzy, you know, but when I saw you on television, I just knew that I was the person you were talking about. So, what can I do for you?"

"Well, actually, a lot," said Miss Westminster. "You see . . ." She stopped. Out of the corner of one eye she had seen something move. She pulled back a branch of the closest plant. Yes—over there in the corner of the dining room, something *was* moving. She pulled back another branch.

"Is anything wrong?" asked Mr. Spaghetti Man.

"I'm not sure," said Miss Westminster. "I just have a funny feeling, that's all—and there's somebody out there watching us."

"Who could it be?" asked Mr. Spaghetti Man nervously.

"I'm not sure of that either," said Miss Westminster.

She pulled back another branch and saw something else moving in another corner of the darkened restaurant. She stood up and walked around the table, pulling back different branches and looking out into the darkness.

"There *is* somebody out there," she whispered to Mr. Spaghetti Man.

"It's probably just some of the other customers," said Mr. Spaghetti Man. "This restaurant is supposed to have a very good reputation." But his voice was quivering.

"Well, I suppose so," said Miss Westminster. She sat down again at the table.

Then the branches slowly parted, and the waiter stepped inside with two steaming platters of spaghetti and meatballs.

"Oh, that does smell deli—" began Mr. Spaghetti Man.

But Miss Westminster jumped up and screamed, *"Aaaaaiiiiieeeee,"* knocking the platters of spaghetti and meatballs out of the hands of the waiter and onto the head of Mr. Spaghetti Man. He now looked just like the monster of the legend!

"It's him!"

84

"It's him!"
"It's him!"
"It's him!"
"It's him!"
"It's him!"
"It's him!"

Peering through the branches of the big plants were the GAFIA, the SSS, the Pasta Nostra, Mad Mary and her Anti-Terrorist Squad, the reporters, Smilin' Jack and the Eleven P.M. News Team from WYUK, and the girls!

CHAPTER FOURTEEN

Head for the Hills!

"Run, Mr. Spaghetti Man, run!" screamed Miss Westminster. "Head for the hills!"

As the GAFIA, the SSS, the Pasta Nostra, Mad Mary and her Anti-Terrorist Squad, the reporters, Smilin' Jack and the Eleven P.M. News Team from WYUK, and the girls lunged for Mr. Spaghetti Man, Miss Westminster began beating them off with her umbrella, but she was soon swept away by the throng still shouting, *"It's him! It's him! It's him! It's him! It's him! It's him! It's him!"*

She finally found herself inside the kitchen with the waiter, who was hiding behind a big pot of spaghetti.

"What's happening?" asked the waiter in a shaky voice. He had lost his Italian accent and his moustache was now hanging from his upper lip.

"Franco!" said Miss Westminster. "Is that you?"

Franco bowed his head. "Yes," he mumbled.

"Was that you on the gondola too?" asked Miss Westminster.

"Yes," said Franco.

"But why?" asked Miss Westminster.

Franco looked up. "I had to know what was going on," he said. "After all, I have a stake in what happens to the spaghetti industry too!"

Suddenly, the door to the kitchen flew open and Mad Mary was silhouetted against the dim light. "All right, Westminster, I'm back from Albany!" she shouted. "Where are you hiding that terrorist?"

Franco crouched lower behind the big pot of spaghetti.

"I'm not hiding him, Mad Mary," said Miss Westminster. "Anyway, he's not a terrorist!"

"Don't tell me he's not a terrorist!" said Mad Mary. "I've heard stories about him for years!"

"Well, if you knew about him before," said Miss Westminster, "then why haven't you tried to capture him?"

"Because I always thought they were talking about Franco," said Mad Mary, "until I heard you talking to the *real* Spaghetti Man on the telephone."

Franco shivered behind the big pot of spaghetti.

"You ought to be ashamed of yourself," said Miss Westminster, "listening in on telephone conversations like that!"

"Yeah, I am!" said Mad Mary with a grin. "Now, where is he?"

"I don't know," said Miss Westminster. "He was with me at a table in the center of the restaurant until you people showed up."

Just then, the GAFIA, the SSS, the Pasta Nostra, the reporters, Smilin' Jack and the Eleven P.M. News Team from WYUK, and the girls appeared behind Mad Mary and her Anti-Terrorist Squad. They all had mean expressions on their faces.

"Girls, girls," shouted Miss Westminster, "I am so glad to see you. I thought I had lost you!"

Fredonia stepped out in front of Mad Mary. "Okay, Miss Westminster," she said menacingly, "what have you done with Mr. Spaghetti Man?"

"Yeah!" echoed the other girls.

"Yeah!" echoed everybody else.

"You mean *you* didn't capture him either?" cried Miss Westminster.

"No!" shouted everybody.

"Well, I don't have him," said Miss Westminster. "I suppose this means that he escaped." She smiled. "I hope you never catch him!"

"Oh, we'll catch him all right," said Mad Mary. "I have just returned from Albany with the latest in anti-terrorist hardware. We will comb this valley and the mountains beyond and I won't rest until I've brought in this Mr. Spaghetti Man. Come on, men!"

Mad Mary and her Anti-Terrorist Squad rushed out of the kitchen, followed closely by the GAFIA, the SSS, the Pasta Nostra, the reporters, Smilin' Jack and the Eleven P.M. News Team from WYUK, and the girls.

"Whew!" said Franco. "Thank heavens Mad Mary didn't see me!"

Miss Westminster turned. "Come on!" she said. "You must help me find Mr. Spaghetti Man before those vigilantes do!"

Franco hesitated. "On one condition," he said.

"What's that?" asked Miss Westminster.

"If you'll let me wear my disguise," said Franco. "Mad Mary would ruin me if she ever found out I was on the opposite side!"

Miss Westminster sighed. "Oh, all right," she said.

Outside the restaurant, gondolas equipped with searchlights and machine guns patrolled the murky waters of the canals. Miss Westminster and Franco hid in the shadows.

While the gondoliers sang "O Solo Mio," Mad Mary shouted through a bullhorn, *I know you're hiding out there, Mr. Spaghetti Man! I know you're somewhere along the canals! Come on out and surrender!*

"Be careful," said Miss Westminster to Franco. "Don't get caught in one of the searchlights. Mad Mary and her Anti-Terrorist Squad might mistake you for Mr. Spaghetti Man!"

"Oh, no," said Franco.

Miss Westminster and Franco began feeling their way along the edge of the buildings.

"Where are we going?" whispered Franco.

"Mr. Spaghetti Man unknowingly gave me a clue that I have revealed to no one until now," said Miss Westminster. "He said that he lives in the mountains above Little Indian—*next to a little babbling brook!*"

"Oh, that must be Little Indian Babbling Brook," said Franco.

"Do you know the way?" asked Miss Westminster excitedly.

"Sure," said Franco. "I used to play up there when I was a kid."

"Well, what are we waiting for?" said Miss Westminster. "Come on!"

"How will we get to the other side of Little Indian?" said Franco. "It used to be easy, but with all these canals now, you can hardly get around."

"I hadn't thought of . . . Look!" said Miss Westminster, pointing. "There's an empty gondola tied up just down the canal. We can take that!"

Quietly, Miss Westminster and Franco made their way to the moored gondola and got in. Miss Westminster grabbed the pole and pushed the gondola out into the canal.

"We'll use the narrow back canals," said Miss Westminster. "That way maybe nobody will see us."

"What's that noise?" asked Franco.

Above them hovered one of Mad Mary's patrol helicopters. It was also equipped with searchlights and machine guns!

But Miss Westminster pushed the gondola behind a building before the searchlights caught them.

Slowly, Miss Westminster maneuvered the gondola through the narrow back canals. Finally, they reached the other side of Little Indian and Miss Westminster tied up the gondola to the dock.

"There's a little path leading out of Little Indian that goes straight up to Little Indian Babbling Brook," said Franco. "Very few people know about it. We should probably take that!"

But out of nowhere, another one of Mad Mary's armed helicopters appeared above them and caught them in its searchlight.

"It's Gert Westminster and the waiter from the Little Indian Secluded Italian Restaurant," boomed Mad Mary's voice from the helicopter. *"They're heading for Mr. Spaghetti Man! Cut'em off!"*

"Oh dear, oh dear!" said Miss Westminster. "That woman is everywhere! What are we going to do?"

"Come on!" said Franco. "This way!"

Miss Westminster and Franco started up the steep slope toward Little Indian Babbling Brook and the place where they thought they'd find Mr. Spaghetti Man.

The armed patrol helicopter continued to hover overhead, its searchlights seeking them out, but the underbrush was thick enough for them to be able to stay out of its beam.

Soon, though, other armed patrol helicopters had joined the first helicopter, their searchlights dancing over the thick vines that covered the path to Little Indian Babbling Brook.

Mad Mary's voice boomed again from one of the hovering helicopters: *"I know you're in there, Gert. I'd sure hate to waste all these anti-terrorist air-to-ground missiles, but I can see you're going to force me to!''*

"Oh, my goodness," said Miss Westminster, "she's going to waste us!"

"Just keep running," said Franco. "Maybe she'll miss us!"

"I wonder if they're heat-seeking missiles," said Miss Westminster.

"I don't know," said Franco. "Why do you ask?"

"Because I'm getting awfully hot," said Miss Westminster, "and they'd find me in a minute!"

"Just keep your cool," said Franco, "and try not to think about it!"

On and on they plunged through the darkness. Above them, Mad Mary's armed patrol helicopters continued to hover, their searchlights still unable to penetrate the thick tangle of vines.

Then from the left side of the trail came the unmistakable sounds of machetes. *Chop! Chop! Chop! Chop! Chop!*

"Oh, my goodness," said Miss Westminster, "I've seen enough jungle movies in my day to know that we are about to be in serious trouble!"

"What's wrong now?" whispered Franco.

But Miss Westminster said nothing. Instead, she stopped and peered through the thick underbrush. "I was right," she finally whispered. "There *are* people chopping their way through this jungle!"

"Who are they?" asked Franco.

"My girls," said Miss Westminster with a lump in her throat, "and behind them, the GAFIA, the SSS, the reporters, Smilin' Jack and the Eleven P.M. News Team from WYUK, and . . . *who are those other people?''*

Franco looked. "I don't believe it," he said. "It's Little Indian's infamous master criminals, Grannie Caster and Her All-Girl Gang!"

"What?'' screamed Miss Westminster. "That woman has been causing me trouble all over the state of New York and I'm sick of it! She has a lot to answer for!"

Miss Westminster started to plunge through the thick tangle of jungle vines, but Franco pulled her back.

"There's no time for personal vendettas," he said.

90

Miss Westminster thought for a minute. "You're right," she said. "I don't know what came over me. Our first obligation is to Mr. Spaghetti Man. But how did that awful woman get here?"

"Anytime there's something really worth going after," said Franco, "Grannie Caster and Her All-Girl Gang go after it!"

"Oh, can you imagine what this world would be like if *she* gained control of the spaghetti industry?" cried Miss Westminster.

"I don't even want to think about it!" said Franco.

"They're gaining on us!" said Miss Westminster. "What are we going to do?"

"I think Little Indian Babbling Brook is somewhere to our right," said Franco. "If we could make it to the brook, then maybe we could *swim* to Mr. Spaghetti Man's cabin!"

"Well, come on," said Miss Westminster, "what are we standing here for?"

Splash! Splash! Splash! Splash! Splash!

"What's that noise?" said Franco.

Miss Westminster peered through the underbrush on her right. "It's the Pasta Nostra in their gondolas," she said. "They've turned Little Indian Babbling Brook into Little Indian Babbling Canal!"

With Mr. and Mrs. Presidente in the lead, an armada of gondolas was making its way upstream. Everyone was standing and singing "O Solo Mio."

"There are people on both sides of us!" said Miss Westminster.

"And above us, Mad Mary and her Anti-Terrorist Squad in their armed patrol helicopters," added Franco.

"We must charge on, for Mr. Spaghetti Man is *ahead* of us," said Miss Westminster. "We have to reach him first!" She hesitated for a moment. "I only wish I had one of those machetes or one of those gondolas!"

"I have a pair of pasta scissors in my pocket," said Franco. "Would that help?"

"Good heavens, yes, man," said Miss Westminster, "why didn't you say so?"

Franco handed the pasta scissors to Miss Westminster and she began cutting the vines.

Together they plunged on through the darkness.

The thick jungle echoed with the sounds of machetes, splashing gondolas, pasta scissors, and screaming armed patrol helicopters overhead.

Finally, Miss Westminster made one final cut with the pasta scissors and plunged into a clearing.

She took a flashlight out of her purse and shone it straight ahead.

She gasped.

Franco gasped.

In the shadow of a roughly hewn mountain cabin, Mr. Spaghetti Man was standing next to a roughly hewn table. On top of the table was a small potted plant.

"It is I, Mr. Spaghetti Man!" shouted Miss Westminster. "Do not be afraid!"

Mr. Spaghetti Man began to tremble, but he did not move from where he was standing.

Just then a crashing sound came from the left side of where Miss Westminster and Franco were standing. The girls had broken into the clearing too, followed by the GAFIA, the SSS, the reporters, Smilin' Jack and the Eleven P.M. News Team from WYUK, and Grannie Caster and Her All-Girl Gang.

Then from the right side came a splashing sound. The Pasta Nostra gondolas had broken into the clearing and were beginning to dock.

Mad Mary's armed patrol helicopters had also begun landing.

The wind from the helicopters knocked Mr. Spaghetti Man to the ground.

Miss Westminster regained her composure and began running toward him.

Just as she reached him, everyone else started toward him.

"Stay back!" shouted Miss Westminster. *"Nobody, but nobody, touches Mr. Spaghetti Man! I've had it with all of you and I have something to say!"*

Fredonia stepped away from the crowd. "We'll hear you out, Miss Westminster," she said, "but it had better be good!"

Miss Westminster looked at the throng of people before her. *"I have witnessed the near collapse of Western Civilization in these last few days,"* she shouted, *"and it has all been because of greed! You are all going to stand there and listen quietly to Mr. Spaghetti Man's story!"*

There was grumbling in the throng, but nobody moved.

Miss Westminster turned and helped the trembling Mr. Spaghetti Man to his feet.

Mr. Spaghetti Man started to speak. "It has all come—"

"We can't hear you!" cried the crowd.

One of Mad Mary's Anti-Terrorist Squad members rushed forward with a loudspeaker.

"It has all come back to me now," began Mr. Spaghetti Man again. "My recent escape from Little Indian has been such a shock that I now remember everything that has happened to me in these last few years."

"Tell us!" cried the crowd.

"It all started ten years ago," said Mr. Spaghetti Man. "I was a teenager, working in my mama's Italian restaurant in Poughkeepsie. She always served homemade spaghetti, but the Pasta Nostra wanted her to buy packaged spaghetti from them. When she refused, they ran her out of business. She had to turn to a life of crime to support me!"

Miss Westminster gasped. "It's Mama Rosa's son Giorgio!"

The girls gasped too.

"Go on! Go on!" cried the crowd.

"Mama was caught, tried, and convicted of a heinous crime and sentenced to life in the Poughkeepsie Popular Prison for People," continued Mr. Spaghetti Man.

"What happened next?" cried the crowd.

"Well, I vowed in court that day that I would avenge my mama's good name," said Mr. Spaghetti Man, "and destroy the Pasta Nostra!"

"Booooooooooooooooooooo!" cried the Pasta Nostra.

"Aaaaaaaaaaahhhhhhhhhh!" cried the rest of the crowd.

"So I came to the mountains above Little Indian with a plan," continued Mr. Spaghetti Man. "I toiled and toiled and I experimented and experimented, and I guess I became a mad scientist, but it worked, and I am now ready to go back out into the real world with my terrible secret!"

"What is your secret?" cried the crowd.

"Shine the searchlights over here where I'm standing!" cried Mr. Spaghetti Man.

Mad Mary's Anti-Terrorist Squad raced for the armed patrol helicopters and began shining the searchlights at where Mr. Spaghetti Man was standing.

"See this!" shouted Mr. Spaghetti Man. He pointed to the small potted plant on the roughly hewn table.

"Yes!" cried the crowd. *"What is it?"*

"A spaghetti plant!" cried Mr. Spaghetti Man. *"I have invented a plant that grows spaghetti!"*

CHAPTER FIFTEEN

Up in Smoke!

By the dawn's early light—and the searchlights from Mad Mary's armed patrol helicopters—everyone could clearly see the potted spaghetti plant. It sort of looked like a sunflower, but where the sunflower seeds would have been, long white strands of spaghetti dropped almost to the ground.

"You see," continued Mr. Spaghetti Man, pointing to the spaghetti plant, "the spaghetti comes out here. Then you break it off, pop it into a spaghetti pot, cook it for five minutes, and presto, you have the best Italian spaghetti in the world! This one tiny potted spaghetti plant will produce enough spaghetti in a day to feed the entire population of the United States!"

The crowd cheered wildly.

"Brilliant!" cried Miss Westminster. "Your mama will be proud of you!"

That brought tears to Mr. Spaghetti Man's eyes. "She probably doesn't even know I'm still alive," he said with a sob.

"Oh, yes, she does," said Miss Westminster.

"Yeah!" cried the girls.

"We saw her a few days ago," said Fredonia.

"We performed for her," said Merridith.

"I was awful," said Loretta. "It was because I wasn't chewing gum!"

"Really?" said Mr. Spaghetti Man.

"Yeah," said Loretta. "I just can't sing and dance if I'm not—"

"Wait a minute! Wait a minute!" shouted Mad Mary. "Cut out all this sentimental drivel!"

"Yeah!" cried the GAFIA, the SSS, the Pasta Nostra, Smilin'

Jack and the Eleven P.M. News Team from WYUK, and Grannie Caster and Her All-Girl Gang. *"We* want a chance to talk to him!"

"I said, just wait a minute!" repeated Mad Mary. "I haven't decided whether he's a terrorist or not!"

"Look at this innocent face, Mad Mary," said Miss Westminster. "Is this the face of a terrorist?"

"No!" cried the crowd.

Mr. Spaghetti Man smiled innocently.

"Well, he does look kind of innocent," said Mad Mary.

Mr. Spaghetti Man smiled even more innocently.

"That's because he is!" said Miss Westminster.

"Well, I don't know, Gert," said Mad Mary. "I've seen a lot of innocent-looking terrorists in my day!"

"Yeah!" cried the Anti-Terrorist Squad.

Mr. Spaghetti Man stopped smiling.

"You can release him to me, Mad Mary," said Miss Westminster. "I'll take full responsibility for him."

Mr. Spaghetti Man smiled again.

"What about us?" cried the GAFIA, the SSS, the Pasta Nostra, Smilin' Jack and the Eleven P.M. News Team from WYUK, and Grannie Caster and Her All-Girl Gang. "Don't we get a chance to talk to him?"

"Well, I don't . . ." began Miss Westminster.

"Freedom of speech!" cried Mad Mary.

"Oh, all right," said Miss Westminster, "but I am totally angry with all of you. GAFIA, you go first, but hurry up!"

Sammy Smith came forward from the crowd. "If you come with us, Mr. Spaghetti Man," he said, "you'll make a lot of money, because we plan to use your spaghetti plant to take over the spaghetti industry. Then everybody will have to come to us if they want to eat spaghetti!"

"Yea!" cheered the GAFIA.

The reporters took notes furiously.

Merridith hurriedly translated into Basque.

"Okay," said Miss Westminster, "we'll now hear from the SSS. Luger Colt, please come forward!"

Luger Colt strutted to the front of the crowd. "Well, you see," he began, "this-here invasion's coming and we survivalists have to be prepared, you know, so we're offering you a chance to save yourself, Mr. Spaghetti Man, and us too, and don't forget your country, from all those evil outside forces that are coming to get us! We need the strength to fight those evil forces and we can only get that strength through your spaghetti plant. In fact, Mr. Spaghetti Man, the new motto of the SSS is 'Strength through Spaghetti'!''

"Yea!'' cheered the SSS.

The reporters took notes furiously.

Merridith hurriedly translated into Basque.

"We shall now hear from the Pasta Nostra,'' said Miss Westminster. "Will Mr. Presidente please come forward?''

Mr. Presidente stepped to the front of the crowd. "As you all know,'' began Mr. Presidente, "spaghetti is essential to the very soul of the Italian people, and it is because of this that we are asking you to bring your spaghetti plant to Italy, Mr. Spaghetti Man. If you do, we in the Pasta Nostra are prepared to honor you with marble statues in every city, every town, and every village in the entire country!''

"Yea!'' cheered the Pasta Nostra.

The reporters took notes furiously.

Merridith hurriedly translated into Basque.

"It is now the turn of Smilin' Jack and the Eleven P.M. News Team from WYUK,'' said Miss Westminster.

Smilin' Jack stepped forward. "It's simple, Mr. Spaghetti Man,'' he said. "If you come with us, we'll make you a prime-time star! You'll have your own show: 'Ask Mr. Spaghetti Man!' People from all over the world will be able to call in and ask you things they've always wanted to know about spaghetti!''

The reporters took notes furiously.

Merridith hurriedly translated into Basque.

Miss Westminster turned to Mr. Spaghetti Man. "You have heard all four contestants, Mr. Spaghetti Man,'' she said, "and now you have—''

"Wait a minute! Wait a minute!'' shouted Grannie Caster. "Don't me and my girls get a turn?''

"I should say not!'' said Miss Westminster. "After all the heartache and humiliation you have caused me! Besides, your grammar is atrocious!''

Grannie Caster walked up to Miss Westminster.

Miss Westminster felt a shiver go down her spine.

"Can you swim, sister?" asked Grannie Caster.

"Of course I can swim," said Miss Westminster. "I teach swimming at my very prestigious girls' school."

"Then come with me," said Grannie Caster. She led Miss Westminster over to the banks of Little Indian Babbling Canal.

"Why did you do this?" demanded Miss Westminster.

"Because I want to see you swim!" cackled Grannie Caster. She shoved Miss Westminster into the canal. Then she ran back to Her All-Girl Gang and they all began cackling hysterically.

Franco rushed over and helped Miss Westminster out of the canal.

Miss Westminster slowly sloshed back to where Mr. Spaghetti Man was standing; then she looked at the crowd again. Her nostrils were flared and she was breathing heavily. ". . . sixty seconds to make up your mind," she continued through gritted teeth. "Does anybody have a clock?"

Mad Mary rushed up to Miss Westminster with a detonator. "This makes loud ticks just before the bomb goes off," she said.

"Good heavens!" said Miss Westminster.

"Don't worry," said Mad Mary, "there's no bomb attached to it."

"Thank heavens!" said Miss Westminster. She started the detonator.

Tick! Tick! Tick! Tick! Tick!

Mr. Spaghetti man started thinking.

"The tension is unbearable!" said Fredonia.

"Yeah!" said Carla and Marla.

"Ah've jus' never been under so much tension," said Augusta. "Not even in Georgia!"

Tick! Tick! Tick! Tick! Tick!

A reporter from Butte, Montana, rushed up to Mad Mary. "How do you fit into all of this, sister?" he asked.

"Through my diligence," said Mad Mary, "I have brought peace to this valley and to the Little Indian Metropolitan Area. I have forced the New York Legislature to recognize that there really is a terrorist problem in this part of the state, and to that end they have provided me with the money to buy the military hardware that I

98

have used to stabilize this area. I alone am responsible for the tranquility of this valley and of this metropolitan area, because everybody knows that if anyone gets out of line, Mad Mary Magillicuddy will blow that person to smithereens!''

"Yea!'' cheered the Anti-Terrorist Squad.

Tick! Tick! Tick! Tick! Tick! Ding! Blam! Blam! Blam! Blam! Blam! Blam! Blam! Blam! Blam! Blam! Blam!''

Miss Westminster looked up into the sky as Mad Mary's rocket launchers exploded into a dazzling display of fireworks. "I thought you said this thing wouldn't detonate!" she shouted.

Blam! Blam! Blam! Blam! Blam!

"Would you look at that!" said Mad Mary. "Those creeps at that pawn shop in Albany sold me Roman candles instead of missiles. I'll have their heads for this!"

Blam! Blam! Blam! Blam! Blam!

Everyone looked up at the red, white, and blue colors that continued to explode and light up the sky.

"Ooooohhhhh!" cried the crowd.

Blam! Blam! Blam! Blam! Blam!

"Aaaaahhhhh!" cried the crowd.

Suddenly, a huge yellow ball shot up, stayed there for a minute, and then started downward.

"It's heading for us, Mr. Spaghetti Man!" screamed Miss Westminster.

"Watch out!" screamed the girls.

"Watch out!" screamed the GAFIA.

"Watch out!" screamed the SSS.

"Watch out!" screamed the Pasta Nostra.

"Watch out!" screamed Smilin' Jack and the Eleven P.M. News Team from WYUK.

"Watch out!" screamed Grannie Caster and Her All-Girl Gang.

"Watch out!" screamed the reporters.

"Watch out!" screamed Franco.

"Watch out!" screamed Miss Westminster as she shoved Mr. Spaghetti Man out of the way.

"Blaaaaaaaaaaam!

The potted spaghetti plant exploded.

CHAPTER SIXTEEN

Give Our Regards to Broadway!

Mr. Spaghetti Man was uninjured but distraught. "Oh me, oh my!" he said with a sob. "There goes ten years of my life!"

Miss Westminster reached down and helped him up. "What do you plan to do with your life now, Mr. Spaghetti Man?" she asked.

"I guess I'll just go back to being a mad scientist and invent the spaghetti plant all over again," said Mr. Spaghetti Man. "I just hope that Mama doesn't rot in prison while I'm doing it."

Mr. Presidente rushed up. "Was that the only spaghetti plant you had?" he asked breathlessly.

"Yes," said Mr. Spaghetti Man with another sob.

"Did you make any scientific notes?" asked Mr. Presidente.

"No," said Mr. Spaghetti Man. "I'll just have to start all over!"

"Wonderful!" said Mr. Presidente. "I mean . . . that's too bad!"

"I know," said Mr. Spaghetti Man.

"Say," said Mr. Presidente, "I have an idea."

Mr. Spaghetti Man looked up. "What is it?"

"Well, we in the Pasta Nostra forgive and forget," said Mr. Presidente. "We are prepared to use our considerable influence with Warden Wilhelmina at the Poughkeepsie Popular Prison for People to have your mother paroled."

Mr. Spaghetti Man's eyes brightened. "That would be wonderful," he said. Then he frowned. "Why would you do this for me?"

"Of course," continued Mr. Presidente, "we would have to have your promise never to experiment with any more spaghetti plants."

"You've got it," said Mr. Spaghetti Man.

He and Mr. Presidente shook hands.

"You look sad, Mr. Spaghetti Man," said Miss Westminster. "Is there still something wrong?"

"I was just wondering what me and my mama will do after she gets out of prison," said Mr. Spaghetti Man.

"You mean after you learn to speak proper English?" said Miss Westminster.

"Yes," said Mr. Spaghetti Man.

Franco rushed up. "I couldn't help overhearing you, Mr. Spaghetti Man," he said. "You know, I sure could use you and your mama to help me run Franco's Famous Italian Spaghetti Inn and Overnight Campground. It's not every day that two people come along who know almost as much about spaghetti as I do."

"Oh, thank you, thank you!" said Mr. Spaghetti Man. "This is all so unreal!"

"It is," said Miss Westminster. "It really is!"

"Yeah!" cried the girls.

Miss Westminster turned.

The girls had rushed over to where Miss Westminster was standing. They all started hugging each other and having a tearful reunion.

"How could we have been so foolish?" said Fredonia.

"Yeah," said Loretta. "The Pasta Nostra doesn't really need to control any more spaghetti!"

"We really never thought there'd be an invasion," said Carla and Marla with a sob. "We don't know why we sided with the SSS."

"We were overcome by GAFIA greed!" cried Merridith.

"Ah've jus' never been so greedy in my entire life," said Augusta. "Not even in Georgia!"

"Oh, girls, girls," cried Miss Westminster as she drew them around her, "I hope that nothing like this ever happens again!"

"I just want to go back to good old Elizabeth, New Jersey, Miss Westminster," said Loretta with a sob.

"Us too!" cried the rest of the girls.

Miss Westminster looked around. The GAFIA, the SSS, the Pasta Nostra, the reporters, Smilin' Jack and the Eleven P.M. News Team from WYUK, Grannie Caster and Her All-Girl Gang, Mad

101

Mary and her Anti-Terrorist Squad, Franco, and Mr. Spaghetti Man had all begun the trek back down the mountain to Little Indian. "Well, I guess we might as well," she said, "now that our plans for a career on Broadway have been shattered."

"Hello!"

Everybody looked up. A little old man was staring at them.

"What do you want?" demanded Miss Westminster. "Can't you see that we are having a tearful reunion?"

The little old man bowed his head and started to turn away.

"Wait!" said Merridith. "It's the California reporter's Basque grandfather!" She frowned. "I didn't know he knew any English!"

"Oh, well, then, how do you do?" said Miss Westminster. "What may we do for you?"

"I am a struggling playwright," said the Basque grandfather. "Last night, by the light of the moon, I was driven to write a magnificient musical based on the life of Mr. Spaghetti Man."

"Really?" said Miss Westminster.

"Really?" said the girls.

"Really," said the Basque grandfather. "And I want to present it to you in appreciation of your excellent Basque translations of this very moving International Italian Spaghetti Summit Meeting!"

Merridith beamed.

"How nice," said Miss Westminster.

"How nice," said the girls.

"That's not all," continued the Basque grandfather. "I want you all to play the most important roles and I want to produce it myself!"

"How absolutely incredible!" cried Miss Westminster. "I can't believe this is happening!"

"Broadway, here we come!" cried the girls.

The Basque grandfather looked puzzled. "No, no," he said, "we're not opening in New York, we're opening in Nome, Alaska!"